Guardian Health Diagnosis: M-100

Paul Humnick

Chapter 1
M-100

I got into my car and scanned-in. "Hello, Hailey."

"Good evening, Dave."

"What's the quickest route home this evening?" I asked.

"Route 2 has an estimated drive time of 23 minutes," she responded.

I pulled out of the parking lot and headed for the freeway. "Where's Monika?"

"She is at the Bluff Creek Station."

"Connect me."

Monika's face appeared on the dash monitor. "Hi, Davey. On your way home already? How was your day?"

"Hi, honey. It was fine. I was at the clinic for my annual exam this morning, so I didn't get as much work done as I hoped to. You got off work on time for a change. How was your day?"

"Fine. We started testing the latest release of the Bio-chip today, which is exciting. The train is just pulling in; I should be home by 6:15. What's for dinner?"

"Is it really my turn again? I'll have to give it some thought. See you at home."

As I merged into traffic I was thinking about the quarterly report that was due on Friday. I figured I could put in a good two hours on it after supper assuming there weren't any interruptions.

"Hailey, any messages?"

"You are out of milk," she answered.

Not again! Two visits from Net Masters and the notification system still had a bug in it. I knew I would regret letting Monika talk me into buying that Net Connex refrigerator. "Hailey, please delete that message. I bought milk on Saturday."

"Message has been saved and notification has been rescheduled."

"No! I said 'delete,' not 'save'!" Why did we need a high-tech refrigerator anyway? And what's wrong with an old-fashioned shopping list? With only two of us at home, it's not like we can't figure out what food we need to have on hand. But I was stuck with it now. "Contact Net Masters and schedule another appointment."

A couple of minutes later Hailey announced, "The first appointment available is Thursday morning at 9:45. Confirm?"

"Yes, confirm," I answered. Then I said to myself, "And if they can't get it to work this time I'm going to have it disconnected from the Net, and I'll figure out for myself when I need to buy milk."

That was an idle threat. I knew Monika would never let me get away with it. She was the techie in our family and could probably fix the problem herself. But the refrigerator was only three months old and was still under warranty, so I insisted that the manufacturer should be responsible for repairing it. But after two unsuccessful attempts I was frustrated. "Hailey, disable the Net Connex notification system."

"I'm afraid I can't do that, Dave."

"Why not, Hailey?"

"Disabling the notification system requires a local scan-in."

"Okay, okay. I'll take care of it when I get home. Are there any . . ."

Hailey interrupted, "Warning! You are exceeding the speed limit by seven miles per hour."

I backed off the accelerator and told myself to calm down. It's just a refrigerator. I didn't need another fine from Guardian Transit for speeding. "Are there any other messages?" I asked.

"You have a priority 1-C message from Guardian Health."

That would be the results of my health exam. I was expecting another good report this year. Dr. Steele said I appeared to be in excellent health, and I told him I felt great. I couldn't remember the last time I had been sick. Since a priority 1-C message required identity verification, I decided to wait until I got home to view it.

It was nearly 6:00 when I arrived home. Stepping into the house, it felt a little too warm for my liking. As I walked over to the refrigerator to see what I could find for supper I asked Hailey, "What is our energy balance?"

"There are 13 kilotherms remaining," Hailey responded.

"Wonderful," I thought. Monika's energy usage plan was working well. We could afford a little more comfort this evening without exceeding our daily energy expenditure. "Lower temperature three degrees and set humidity to 30 percent," I told Hailey.

"Temperature will be lowered three degrees. Humidity will be set to 30 percent," she replied.

I found some leftover spaghetti sauce in the fridge and put it on the stove to warm up along with a pot of water for the pasta. As I was making the salad I remembered the message from the clinic. "Hailey, access Guardian Health messages."

"You have a priority 1-C message. Please scan-in and verify identity."

I decided to take it in the kitchen. Priority 1-C meant it was "for your eyes and ears only," but I wasn't concerned if Monika came home while I was listening. I walked over to the monitor and placed my left hand under the scanner, then placed my right index finger on the fingerprint reader.

"Identity confirmed. Message ready."

"Play message."

Dr. Steele came on the screen. That struck me as odd. All my previous results had been reported by a nurse. "Hello, David. I'm sure you're wondering why I'm the one contacting you this time. I'm sorry, but I have bad news. The deep tissue scan came out positive for malignancy. You will need to schedule a follow-up appointment within 72 hours. We'll run a higher resolution scan to verify the results, but our diagnostic department is currently operating with a three percent margin of error, so the diagnosis will not likely change. You have been designated as M-100. The malignancy is in your pancreas, but the cell damage . . ."

He continued on, but I felt like I had been transported to a different universe. There must be some mistake. I was 54 years old. I took good care of myself and I was a bit of a health food fanatic. I had a deep tissue scan a year earlier and everything was fine. Now I was being told I had advanced malignancy. How could that be? Could this really be happening?

Monika walked in. "Mmmm, smells like Italian food tonight. Want help with the salad? Is that Dr. Steele I see?"

Dr. Steele's message was still playing. ". . . we should start treatment as soon as possible. If you will scan-in, I'll grant you Level 2 access to the National Health Database. We can discuss all of this further at your next appointment. Before we meet, take a few minutes to look over the attached timetable. I'll see you soon."

"Treatment! What kind of treatment? What's going on?"

I told Hailey to turn off the stove pads, and then said to Monika, "Let's sit down." We sat together on the couch and I blurted out, "I'm M-100." That's all I said. Monika took my hand, and we sat there for several minutes without saying a word.

"Davey, we have 100 days. Let's make them count. I'll take a leave-of-absence. We can do whatever you want to do, go wherever you want to go."

I appreciated her response. She didn't try to get me to talk about how I was feeling, or worse, try and give me false hope by telling me I could beat this thing. She was an RN and knew what my chances were. She wanted my last few months of life to be as rich and happy as possible. I could think of a dozen things I'd like to do before I died. We could have a great time together. Maybe the kids could join us for part of it. The children! How would my death affect them? I realized instantly that if for no other reason I needed to fight this thing for their sake. Even before I consciously formed that thought, I was aware of something inside of me that was saying, "Don't give in!" It wasn't something I needed to think over. I knew I would fight.

I put my arm around Monika and gave her a hug. "I need time to think and figure this all out. When I'm satisfied I've exhausted all my options, maybe I'll be ready to have one last fling—or possibly two!"

She smiled and said, "I already knew you would say something like that. I guess I should have thought a bit longer before making such an un-Davidlike suggestion. How about I get supper ready?"

We sat down to eat, but I didn't have much of an appetite. I put on my pragmatic hat and started planning out loud. "We need to tell the kids, but I want to wait until after my next appointment. If I remember right, we have to submit our preliminary documents to Guardian Estate by Day 90. I'd appreciate some help filling those out. We should start discussing treatment options."

Actually there wasn't that much to discuss. As far as I knew, there weren't many treatment options available for malignancy. The disease had only started appearing within the last five years or so, and not much progress had been made toward a cure.

Monika's voice sounded a bit energized when I mentioned treatment. "Dave, there are clinical trials going on with stem cell therapy. They've had some successes recently treating malignancy. I can see what I can do to get you accepted. I could come with you to your next appointment and discuss it with Dr. Steele. If you want to fight this, then let's do it together."

I hadn't kept up on the latest developments in malignancy treatment. It had been several years since I remember hearing about stem cell therapy on the news. They had made great gains in treating a number of types of cancer. But research on frequency generators showed much more promise, and when Generator Prime was finally approved by the Ministry of Health, cancer treatment was revolutionized.

I felt somewhat encouraged and as I got up from the table I said, "Thanks, I'd like that. I've got a lot to learn and not much time. I want to get started as soon as I can, while I still feel strong and healthy. I'm going to start by taking a look at the NHD."

"You know I have Level 3 access. I can let you use it. You'd be able to see more information in your medical records and go deeper in your research," Monika offered.

I knew that if she did that she would be breaking the rules, and if she got caught her job would be at risk. "If we tried to open my health records using your digital signature, Guardian Security would detect it immediately. You know you aren't allowed to use Level 3 access for personal reasons—even for research. Besides, there's more than enough public information available to keep me busy for weeks."

"Yes, I know. I just wanted you to know that it's available if you want to use it."

"Thanks. But there's no point in risking your career. You might need it."

She gave me a long look, but didn't say any more.

Monika cleaned up the supper dishes and I sat down at the desk. I told Hailey to reopen Dr. Steele's message.

"Ready," she said.

I placed my hand under the scanner and said, "Download the NHD access code." The scanner flashed briefly and my Bio-chip was updated. "Open the National Health Database." The NHD homepage came up. The first thing I did was to navigate to my recent exam report. Most of the information was meaningless to me, but I did want to take a look at my scan results. I selected a graphic, zeroed in on the pancreas, and enlarged it. There were a number of small red blotches visible, which indicated malignant cells. Malignancy was found in my pancreas, but there was no indication that it had begun spreading to other organs, which was a relief.

As I stared at the monitor I wondered to myself, "Why? What caused those cells to become infected?" I knew enough to understand that malignancy was not related to cancer. In the early days people mistakenly associated it with cancerous, malignant tumors, but it was quite different. Malignancy did not cause tumors. It somehow caused damage to normal, healthy cells, which resulted in abnormal degeneration. But that was about all I knew about it.

"Search malignancy," I told Hailey. Google pulled up over 1,300,000 hits. It was going to be a long night.

Chapter 2

Day 99 — Wednesday, May 7th

I took a couple of personal days off of work. I wasn't required to report my diagnosis to my company until Day 60. At that point I would have at most 30 days before I would be released. I wasn't ready to give up my job until I had to—at least that's how I felt right now.

Monika wanted to take the same days off as well, but other than taking time off for the appointment with Dr. Steele on Thursday morning, I asked her not to. I had plenty of reading and research ahead of me, and we could discuss it together in the evening. Besides she was needed at the clinic. The Bio-chip trials were just getting started and there was a lot to do. If she wasn't there, everyone else would have to work that much harder. She agreed, but only if we had the whole evening alone together, and we set the Net to Privacy Mode.

After she left for work I poured myself another cup of coffee. I had gotten less than five hours of sleep the previous night and was beginning to feel drowsy. But my appointment at the clinic was scheduled for tomorrow morning, and I wanted to be well prepared.

I must have gone through over 100 documents on the Net since last evening. Most only required a cursory review, but I read a few of them thoroughly. I began by studying malignancy, but for a layman like me, most of the technical papers were way beyond my ability to comprehend, and what I could understand didn't hold my attention for long. Since it was a relatively new disease, not much research had been done yet, although that was beginning to change. However, I was fascinated by the information on frequency generators and spent most of my time reading about them.

In addition to reams of technical papers, there were a couple of books written about frequency generators in simple language for "Dummies" like me. I bought a digital version of one of the books and didn't want to put it down. I found out that the history of the device dated back almost a hundred years. But development of a modern version began only 20 years ago by Future Health, a private medical device company. The first model, Generator Prime, came on the market 12 years ago, followed by Generator Premier six years later. The latter was the enhanced model that included imaging capability. As soon as the Premier model was released, it proved to be the best diagnostic tool available for cancer. At first it was acquired by large, private hospitals in the major cities, but after it proved its worth, Guardian Health made a push to get them in its hospitals and clinics nationwide. There was plenty of political support for that initiative, but back then our country was in the midst of an economic crisis, ironically due in part to the large number of people receiving cancer treatment with the Generator, which was primarily being paid for by the national health care system. But now that the economy was recovering, they couldn't seem to install the machines fast enough.

There was endless chatter on the Net about Generator Premier. It was a resounding success in treating, even curing, many cancers and there were numerous individuals and groups advocating it. There were hundreds of others who shared their personal stories of overcoming cancer. On the other side there were also quite a few groups and individuals attempting to sound the alarm. They ranged from concern over the exorbitant financial burden being placed on taxpayers, to fears of unknown health risks and latent side-effects from exposure to the Generator. There was also the occasional rant about it being used as a mind-control device by the government. Good grief!

As I drank my coffee I started working my way through some of the resources I had marked for further study. They were all related to frequency generators. In the next few hours I went through over a dozen medical journals and scholarly papers, and was impressed by the amount of data that showed Generator Premier and Prime to be effective and extremely safe. There were virtually no side-effects. The exception being that occasionally generators killed too many cancer cells in a session, which resulted in a healing crisis called a Herxheimer reaction, giving the patient flu-like symptoms as the body tried to deal with so many dead cells at once. And there were some precautions for people who had medical implants, like pace-makers, insulin synthesizers, or brain wave regulators. But that was it. It was an amazing device and I wondered if it held any promise for curing malignancy.

I only found a couple of respectable resources that describe how the Generator might be used to treat malignancy. Most of the research into malignancy treatment focused on stem cell therapy. A couple of universities were involved in research and clinical studies with stem cell treatment of malignancy, but they were woefully underfunded and progress was slow. However, Nucell, the largest private stem cell research facility in the nation, was pouring hundreds of millions into this project. I added their name to my notes to discuss with Dr. Steele tomorrow.

By mid-afternoon I had fallen asleep on the couch. When I woke up, Monika had arrived home and had supper waiting. I must have talked non-stop for an hour and a half, jumping from topic to topic and sounding like a kid who just visited his first holographic arcade. When I finally got up to make some coffee, Monika saw her opportunity.

"I haven't seen you this worked up in a long time. But it's exciting stuff, isn't it? So, is there anything left to discuss or have you already covered everything?"

"That was only the first half of my lecture. I'll try and make the second half a bit more cohesive," I said teasingly. "I think what I really want to do is get out and take a walk. Let's leave the dishes and enjoy the cool evening."

"Let's go. I'll be ready in ten minutes. That's just enough time for you to take care of the dishes," she said as she headed for the bedroom.

"Thanks a lot," I said as I started to clear the dishes from the table.

As we were putting on our shoes, someone was calling. "Should I take it?" I asked Monika.

She sighed and said, "I see you forgot to switch to Privacy Mode like we agreed. You had a few things on your mind I guess. Hailey, who is calling?"

Hailey responded, "Julia."

"Oops! I bet she's calling about to find out how the quarterly report is coming along. I should have contacted her. I better take it," I said.

"Hailey, connect us."

Julia's smiling face appeared on the monitor. "Hello, David. And hello, Monika. How are you doing? I hope I caught you at a good time," Julia said.

"Hi, Julia. Sorry I didn't call you today. We're fine. We were just about to step out for a little exercise. Are you calling about the report?" I asked.

"I just wanted to see if you'll be able to finish it by Friday. If not, I'll need to find someone else to help me with it."

"I plan to finish it tomorrow and bring it in on Friday morning."

"So you'll be at the divisional meeting then?" she asked.

"Yes, I'll be there. Julia, could we have lunch sometime early next week?"

She gave me that "is something up" look and said jokingly, "If you're buying, I'm available on Monday. Otherwise you'll have to wait until Thursday."

"Monday sounds good, but didn't I buy last time? I need a bigger expense account!"

"So, is this a business lunch?" she asked.

"Not exactly. Looks like it will come out of my own pocket."

"That's an old expression. It had something to do with real money, didn't it?" she said and laughed. "See you Friday morning. I'll let you get out and enjoy the evening. Goodbye."

"Thanks. Goodbye," I said and told Hailey to disconnect.

Monika was curious. "Are you going to talk to Julia about the diagnosis?" she asked as we headed out the door.

"Yes," I said. "I trust her like a sister. She'll keep it confidential, and I'm not putting her on the spot, since she isn't under any obligation to report our conversation to the company.

You know what I think about her. I've never worked for anyone who takes such a personal interest in the people who work for her. I almost feel obligated to tell her about this."

"Lucky you. I wouldn't mind a boss like that," Julia said trying to sound pitiful. "But I understand, and I think it's the right thing to do."

We walked and I talked a little more about my research. I told her I was interested in learning more about stem cell therapy and intended to bring it up with Dr. Steele. Then we started to discuss the children and how we would break the news to them. Tomorrow was going to be another full day.

Chapter 3

Day 98 — Thursday, May 8th

Monika and I arrived at the clinic just before 8:00 a.m. and I was taken directly to Imaging. I changed into a hospital gown and the technician took me into the Generator room. I had seen the device before, but after all my research I was more observant this time and looked it over carefully. There wasn't much to see. The base was like a large bed, and above it was an arm that extended out over the width of the base. The arm could move from the head to the foot of the bed, and was controlled by a computer in the corner of the room. Outwardly it didn't look like anything that could be used to cure cancers and other diseases. But I knew that it was capable of producing powerful radio waves that easily penetrated the human body. I had learned that when it is used for treating cancer it requires the patient to be injected with a solution of nanoparticles, but for diagnostic use it functioned more like a sophisticated X-ray machine—only without any harmful radiation.

The technician spoke, "You forgot to scan-in. Is everything alright?"

"Sorry. Yes, I'm fine." I walked over to the computer to scan-in and said, "I've been reading about the Generator lately, and I guess my mind was wandering. It's a marvelous invention, isn't it?"

"It's curing cancers. That goes beyond marvelous in my opinion," the technician replied.

I walked back, and as lay on the bed I asked somewhat rhetorically, "I wonder if it will be able to cure malignancies someday?"

"I wouldn't be surprised. I understand that they're working on it. But just think how long it took to find a cure for cancer. Okay, are you ready?" she said as she sat down at the computer.

"Ready," I said.

"This is going to take about 20 minutes. Hold as still as possible, otherwise you'll be back here tomorrow," she said and started the scan.

Even though the scan only covered my abdomen it took almost as long as my previous full-body scan, but that must have been because it was set to a higher resolution. After it was finished I got dressed and went back to reception area. Monika and I waited nearly half an hour before a medical assistant led us into Dr. Steele's office.

Dr. Steele came around from behind the desk to shake our hands. "Good morning, David. Glad to see you again, Monika. Have a seat. No, wait. Grab some coffee and Danish first. It's over there on the table."

We took him up on his offer and then sat down. Dr. Steele had been my doctor for 15 years and we knew each other well. He was always concise, thorough, and candid with me. Best of all, he was very personable and I felt very comfortable with him. He was a good listener, but I had learned to keep my comments and questions short and to the point. "Good morning, Dr. Steele. What do you say we get right to it? Let me have the full report," I said hoping to avoid any "how are you handling this" type questions he might have.

Dr. Steele looked at me for a few seconds. "Okay, Dave. I'll put my charming bedside manner routine aside and try and lay it out is clearly and quickly as I can, and then I'll let you ask your questions. I can see that you've already accessed your exam report on the NHD. Most of the numbers on the report are confusing and, in my opinion, not worth worrying about. The graphics tell the story pretty well, and we'll have a much clearer picture this afternoon when the high resolution scan results are available. I don't expect to find that other organs have been infected, but it's possible. Malignancy is still a big mystery, but it is fairly predictable, especially in a case like yours where there are no other complications. It typically strikes one organ, but it can spread to surrounding organs. You saw the infected areas of your pancreas as red blotches on the graphics. Cell degeneration occurs gradually followed by apoptosis, that is, cell death. Generally, organ function is only mildly compromised until late in Phase Three when large numbers of cells begin to die. A healthy individual's immune system can handle a certain amount of cells dying, but as more and more cells die, the immune system gets overloaded. It's at that point some physical discomfort begins."

"Is that due to a Herxheimer reaction?" I asked.

"Very good. Have you been instructing him, Monika, or is he self-taught?" asked Dr. Steele.

"He's been spending way more time with the Net lately than with me. I'm learning a lot from him this week," she said and gave me a smile.

Dr. Steele continued, "Once you start to lose organ function in Phase Four, there is little more that can be done. In your case, you would likely have less than two weeks to live from that point. Suffering will be minimal toward the end and we can control most of the pain."

"I'm not sure I'm ready to discuss that part yet," I said.

"I understand. Let's move on to treatment options. A transplant is your best option and I've already put you on the waiting list. But realistically, it is unlikely to happen. The list is too long and we don't have enough time. Another approach revolves around immunotherapy and consists of weekly treatment with the Generator as well as medication."

"I read a couple of papers on using the Generator for immune system therapy. Can you tell me more?" I asked.

"I doubt I can tell you more than you've already learned. You probably understand the basic workings of the Generator. It uses a formula of cycles per second, or Hertz, amplitude, or intensity, and duration. I like to illustrate using a piano. It can produce 88 notes, each one with its own unique frequency or wave length. You can play a note loudly or softly; that's amplitude or intensity. You can play a note briefly or sustain it; that's duration. Play three or four notes together, as in a chord, and multiple frequencies are produced simultaneously. The Generator is capable of producing millions of individual frequencies, combine any number of them, and vary their intensity and duration. Just think about the number of permutations that are possible using all those variables."

He continued, "Of course the challenge is combining those variables into a formula that has the desired effect. In the case of cancer treatment, the goal is to kill cancer cells while not harming healthy cells. Some of those formulas have been discovered, and when used in conjunction with nanoparticle injections, they are successfully curing many types of cancer. However, with malignancy we don't want to kill cells that are infected—they are already dying. We need a different approach. Current Generator research is two pronged: first, finding a formula to stimulate cell repair, essentially reviving them and second, finding formulas that will increase the body's natural immune response, which can slow down the spread of the infection. So far more progress has been made in the latter approach."

"Do they think they can find a way to bring dead cells back to life?" I asked in disbelief.

"No, not dead cells. The goal is to revive damaged cells, to help sick cells regenerate. This is not just theory. It has been shown that plants can be affected, positively and negatively, by external stimuli such as sound frequencies. Frequency therapy has also been effective on In vitro animal cells in laboratory experiments. I don't keep up on the research, but I understand that they have been conducting experiments on live animals in Europe for some time. Still, we are probably years away from human experimentation—at least in the U.S."

"So you're recommending the immune strengthening approach for me?"

"I want you to start next week. You'll need weekly sessions for the first month or so. We'll see how you respond and make adjustments as necessary after that. The final treatment option has to do with stem cell therapy. Have you read about that?" Dr. Steele asked.

"A little. Most of the information I found dealt with using stem cell therapy to treat cancer and other conditions, but not malignancy," I answered.

"That's right. The Generator is so successful at treating cancer that research into treating cancer with stem cells was stopped. Then a couple of years after malignancy came on the scene, stem cell research was intensified with renewed vigor. There are several clinical trials in progress and I've saved the best news for last," he said smiling at us. "I've contacted a former colleague of mine, Brandon, who now works at Nucell. They are conducting clinical trials in conjunction with the university here and they are willing to fast track your application. If you want to proceed we should submit the application right away. If you are accepted, you could start within three to four weeks. It's your best shot, Dave."

I was stunned. Monika couldn't contain herself. "Dave, I can't believe it! There must be a God. I've been asking Him for exactly that, acceptance into a stem cell trial. There's hope now. We . . . I mean you, have to go for it."

I agreed instantly. I felt like this was my one chance. I jumped to my feet and practically shouted, "Yes! Let's get the application in today."

"Alright. We can take care of it right away. I know this is exciting, but I want you to understand that there's a chance you won't qualify. But Brandon tells me the trials are going full throttle and they are still trying to fill their quota for M-100 cases. Based on what I know, you have an excellent chance of getting in. I'm really happy for you, Dave. Now it's your turn. What questions do you have for me on that MiNDi you've been focusing all your attention on?" asked Dr. Steele.

I scrolled through my notes one last time and said, "I think you covered the important ones. I've been checking them off one by one."

He stood up and walked around his desk. "Okay. I'll have someone help you get going on the application. The clinic needs to provide most of it the information, so your part shouldn't take too long. We can submit it this afternoon. I've got a couple of prescriptions for you that you should start taking today. Do you want to pick them at the pharmacy downstairs or near your home?"

"Near to home would be better."

"I'm including a prescription for sleeping pills. You don't have to use them if you don't want to, but it's important to get enough rest. That takes care of it. I'll call you this evening if there is anything further to report once I've seen the scan report. Otherwise, the results should be available on the NHD by 8:00 tonight if you want to take a look. Don't forget to schedule the appointment for your first treatment on your way out."

As we were walking out together I stopped and I looked him in the eye, "Thanks, thanks so much for your help getting me into the clinical trial. I came in feeling like I wasn't up to this. I was even going to ask you about early termination options." As I said that Monika gave me a look of astonishment. "But now I'm full of hope again."

Dr. Steele's smile faded and he looked at me solemnly, "Dave, I hope we never have to have that discussion. I am glad you're hopeful, but let's not celebrate just yet, okay? One day at a time."

We said goodbye, and Monika and I went to start working on the application.

On the drive home I was thinking about what it would be like to participate in a stem cell trial. I didn't know much about it and wanted more information. "I should have asked Dr. Steele about that," I thought. I noticed Monika was not saying anything. "What's on your mind?" I asked.

"Early termination. You never mentioned that to me. Were you planning to let me know before you killed yourself or after?" she said with obvious frustration in her voice.

I knew she had a right to be angry. I just couldn't bring myself to discuss it with her, and I was sorry she had to hear me bring it up for the first time in the doctor's office. "I'm sorry. You have every right to be angry. It's just not an easy topic to bring up. I only wanted to get some information, to know what all my options are. And besides, it's not exactly suicide."

"It isn't? You're the one making the decision to terminate your life prematurely. Just because someone else gives you the injection doesn't mean you aren't responsible."

"Okay, maybe it's a type of suicide. But what if I can't handle the pain or suffering? If I'm going to die anyway, why go through that?" I argued.

"We shouldn't play God. He's the only one who should decide when it's our time to die," she responded.

I was surprised by her answer. We had discussed abortion a few times, but I don't remember ever discussing euthanasia in our 23 years of being together—even when the laws were changed to make it legal in certain cases. "Why is this any different than abortion? You don't oppose that?" I shot back.

"It's not the same. A fetus is not the same as a person. We've had this discussion more than once," she said.

I didn't want to discuss abortion. We had different points of view and neither of us was going to change our stance. I knew I couldn't defend euthanasia though. I had always believed it was wrong just like I believed abortion was wrong, but now that I was facing a potentially painful death, my beliefs were being challenged. Maybe I was a hypocrite, or maybe a coward. "I'm probably both," I thought. I said in a calmer voice, "Okay, I'm not sure what I believe anymore. I need to think about it. I promise to discuss it with you when I'm ready."

She was satisfied. "Good. I know how much stress you're under and that you haven't been sleeping well these last few days. This is by far the hardest thing we've ever faced. We don't need to waste time and energy arguing."

"Monika, you've mentioned God twice today. That's probably more than you have in the last ten years. We used to have some spiritual discussions a long time ago. Are you getting interested in religion again?"

"Aren't you? Haven't you thought about what happens after you die? I know we have no way of knowing, but I'd like to think God exists and maybe we'll be with him after we die."

"Mostly I've been thinking about trying not to die!" I joked. "Seriously, these last few nights when I'm lying in bed at night and it's dark and quiet, I do sometimes wonder about death and what happens afterward. There is something inside that wants to know more, but I don't know where to start."

"Why don't you ask God to help you? If he does exist and if he wants us to believe in him, I think that's a prayer he would probably answer."

I thought about that for a minute and smiling at her said, "Your logic is impeccable as always, Mr. Spock." She gave me an elbow in the ribs. But it did make good sense, and I had already voiced a silent prayer.

When we got home we ate lunch and then sat down together at the desk in the study.

"Ready?" asked Monika.

"Here goes," I said. "Hailey, call Lori." Lori was my 29 year old daughter who lived on the other side of the city about 20 miles from us. Her mother had died from cancer when she was only five. When Monika and I started living together, she was happy to have a mom again. But when she graduated from college and started living with Caleb, she and Monika drifted apart. We talked to each other at least once a week and tried to get together every other month, although it had been less frequent lately.

She came on the screen and smiled when she saw me. "Hi, Lori. How's my girl?" I asked.

"Busy—just like you always are. When are we going to have lunch again? Hi, Mom. How are you?" she asked.

"We'll get together soon, I promise. Do you have a few minutes? I have to talk to you about something important."

She took the news badly. I tried to stay upbeat and concentrate on the good news. When I told her about my chances of getting into a stem cell clinical trial, her mood changed noticeably.

"Caleb's uncle, or maybe it was his cousin, was just in one of those!" she exclaimed. "He was in therapy for about a month, or maybe it was two, I don't know, and they said he's doing really well. He's already been taken off the 'M' scale. He was diagnosed as M-200 about six months ago . . . maybe it was M-100 and it was four months ago, I don't remember. I'll ask Caleb. But he's getting better! You have to get in, Dad, you've just have to."

It was a relief to get through the first call. I hoped Jasmine would handle it as well.

Standing up to stretch I said, "Alright, let's try Jasmine. Hailey, call Jasmine."

Jasmine was our 22 year old daughter. After dropping out of college, she moved to Colorado to pursue her love of skiing, hiking, and camping. She worked as a life-guard and swimming instructor.

The monitor indicated voice mode only as I heard Jasmine answer, "Hi, Dad. I'm at the pool so I'll have to stick to voice mode so I can keep an eye on the swimmers. How's everything with you?" she asked.

"Fair. I'm not sure this is the right time to talk to you if you're that distracted. Do you want to call me back later? I have some important news to tell you."

"Good or bad?" she asked.

"Mostly bad I'm afraid."

"Hold on for a minute," she said.

After a couple of minutes she came back and said, "Okay, I found someone to take over for me for a few minutes, and I stepped outside where it's quiet. Let's hear it and don't sugar coat the bad stuff please."

"No nonsense, get to the point. Did you learn that from me?" I said and then told her the details in the same way I would have liked to hear them. "Those are the facts, Jaz. What do you think?"

"I think it really stinks! My dad has malignancy. I don't want you to die! You don't even sound worried. Are you?"

"I have moments where I get scared. But you know me; something is broken and I want to do everything I can to try and fix it. That's kept me distracted so far. And I can tell you in all honesty that I'm pretty encouraged about the stem cell thing. I just talked to your sister and she said Caleb's uncle or cousin, or maybe it was his grandfather—you know how confused she can get—has malignancy and apparently responded very well to stem cell therapy. So try and think positively about this. Isn't that what you tell me all the time?" I reminded her.

"Why did you go through with those screenings anyway? We've talked about it. You know what I think: they bombard you with dangerous radiation. Just look at the facts. Malignancy is just like radiation poisoning. Haven't you heard that?"

"Jaz, you can't argue with the fact that millions of people have not been harmed by the Generator. Just the opposite, cancers are being cured and lives are being saved. And the Ministry of Health conducted hundreds of tests and approved it without any warnings, more or less."

"Don't get me started on the Ministry of Health, or on the big medical companies for that matter. Do you really believe they have our best interests in mind? They are all . . ." she said as her tone grew angrier.

"Let's not get started on that right now," I pleaded.

She sighed. "I'm sorry. We do know how to push each other's buttons, don't we? I want to talk to you more about this, but I've got to get back in to relieve my sub. If you want to go the stem cell route, I understand. But there are other options. You really need to look at what natural medicine has to offer. You don't like to leave any stone unturned, so at least investigate it. I know people; I have resources; I can help you. Please let me. I love you. Gotta go."

"I love you, too. Give me a call and we'll talk. Bye," I said.

Monika said, "Pure Jasmine. Big brother and corporate America are our enemies. She loves to debate with you. But I can tell that she is scared. You need to talk to her more often in the days ahead. And let her help you, it will make her feel better."

"I will. And I'll be sure and call her more often. If she can't get off work to come here, then I want to visit her soon. I wouldn't mind a trip to the mountains in June!"

"You mean, 'we' don't you. I can get off work," Monika corrected me.

"Yes, we'll both go," I said.

About an hour later as I was reading a paper about stem cell therapy Hailey announced, "Dr. Steele is calling."

"Connect us," I told Hailey.

"David, I see you're at home. Is Monika with you?" he asked.

"She's in the other room. Should I call her?" I asked.

"I have the results of the scan and it would be better to share it with you privately. You can fill her in yourself. The good news is there are no signs that the malignancy has infected any other organs. Unfortunately, we did find some additional infection of the pancreas. It's surprising; there shouldn't have been that much change since your previous scan. I ran the information through the diagnostic algorithms twice and I'm sorry to say that you've been reclassified as M-95."

M-95! Three days of my life just vanished. I was bewildered and discouraged. "Do you think it's because the higher resolution scan is showing more detail?" I asked.

"Not in this case. These spots are large enough that they should have shown up on the previous scan. I wish I could tell you what's going on, but I don't know why those cells suddenly became infected. But don't be too alarmed, Dave. Malignancy will sometimes spread at an accelerated rate for a time and then slow down. The statistical models take all that into account and that's why the 'M' ratings are so reliable. One last thing, Brandon called me and said Nucell received the application and will start processing it right away. He thought you would be notified by next Wednesday or Thursday. Any more questions?"

"No, not right now. I'll try not to worry about it. Thanks for calling," I said and went to tell Monika the news. "Don't worry about it. Ya, right," I said to myself. I think I was going to try one of those sleeping pills tonight.

Chapter 4

Day 94 – Friday, May 9th

I slept soundly and woke up feeling energetic. I was looking forward to being back to work. I had an hour or so before the meeting started so I went to my office to give the quarterly report one last review. Julia stuck her head in the door about 30 minutes later.

"Good morning. Everything ship-shape? Never mind, it always is. We'll start at 9:00 sharp. Are you surprised to see the company survived without you for two days?" she asked. Before I could answer she was on her way down the hall.

The divisional meeting ended up lasting most of the morning. We took a long lunch and then it was time for a meeting with the people in my department. I headed up the customer service operations for our Far East division. We were facing stiff competition in that region, and management wanted to be sure we didn't miss any opportunities to grow our market share there. They were pushing us to improve and expand our operations, and I was feeling the pressure. But I had some talented people in my department, and I thought we were up to the challenge.

I had learned some important lessons about employee relations from my boss, Julia. She showed an interest in everyone who worked for her. She was demanding, but fair. I had worked with her for nine years now, and as I got to know her, the one thing that struck me about her was how she had different priorities than other executives I knew. She would often get to work early, but she was almost always out the door by 5:15. She rarely worked Saturdays and I never saw her at the office on a Sunday. Maybe that had something to do with her religion. She had talked to me more than once about how God came first, then her family, and then her career. I respected her for that and tried to imitate her—at least the part about putting family before my career. I had failed plenty of times though, disappointing my kids and Monika. But we had stuck by each other even through some hard times, and I was pretty happy with how our family got along and cared for one another.

The departmental meeting went longer than I anticipated. As usual, most of the discussion had to do with disagreements on budgetary issues. I tried to listen to everyone's concerns and complaints, but I found my mind wandering frequently. By the time 4:00 rolled around I couldn't concentrate very well, so I suggested we schedule another meeting for the following week. Everyone jumped at the suggestion and the room was empty in less than five minutes. As I sat there by myself taking a few more notes, Julia came in.

"Long meeting. Any problems?" she asked.

"Think you can get us another two or three million for this year's budget?" I asked.

"Is that all? The Central America division asked for five million," she said with a smile. "Are we still on for lunch on Monday?" she asked.

"I'm counting on it," I said.

"I'll look forward to it. Have a good weekend, Dave."

"You, too. See you on Monday."

Chapter 5
Day 91 – Monday, May 12th

I had determined to relax and catch up on some needed rest over the weekend. I had a number of projects that needed to be done around the house, and there were always reports or something else from work to catch up on, but I decided to let them all slide. Instead I sat on the front porch and read my novel in the warm May sun, went for a couple of walks, watched a movie with Monika, and even took a nap. I called my brother, Owen, and told him about my diagnosis. He couldn't believe it. We hadn't talked or seen each other for nearly two years and I think he was feeling guilty for not staying in touch. So was I. We agreed to get together soon.

I called Jasmine on Sunday and she was anxious to talk to me. She had been researching stem cell therapy and thought it was worth a try. She wasn't at all happy that I told her I'd be doing weekly Generator sessions, and she pleaded with me to reconsider. I tried to reassure her that it wasn't risky, but she kept trying to warn me. Finally, I changed the subject and asked about her thoughts on natural remedies. She jumped at the chance to talk with me about it and promised to send me some articles to read. We also talked about her coming to visit us. She was excited and said she'd book a flight as soon as she could arrange time off of work. That gave me something to look forward to, and I started making plans for our time together.

I hadn't been feeling particularly stressed out, but I guess I must have been because after a relaxing weekend I felt like a different person on Monday morning. "If I live long enough, I need to remember to slow down and enjoy life more," I told myself. I had told myself that more than once in the past, but every time I quickly slipped back into the old routine. This time, if I had the chance, I was going to make a real effort.

I got to the office and spent most of the morning reworking the budget. We had scheduled another departmental meeting for Thursday, and I had several ideas on how to restructure operations in order to economize for the remainder of the budget cycle. Just before noon, I walked over to Julia's office. Her door was open as usual, but I knocked to get her attention.

"Are you busy?" I asked.

"I'm just about finished. Let's meet at reception in ten minutes," she said.

"I'll see you there," I said and headed for the elevator.

She was on time as usual, and as we walked to the restaurant she asked me how Monika and the kids were doing, and I asked about her children. After we got to the restaurant, found a table, and ordered, she looked at me and said, "You've piqued my curiosity. I'm anxious to find out why you wanted to have lunch."

"I needed to discuss something confidential with you. I'd like to ask that you don't say anything about it to anyone else, at least for the next few weeks."

"Okay, you can trust me."

"I know. You've never let me down. Last week I had a health exam. I was diagnosed as M-100," I said and paused.

Julia looked at me and then stared down at the table for several seconds. "I had to deal with this in my family. It's dreadful, awful. I'm so sorry. But knowing you, you're going to fight it, right? It's not an automatic death sentence no matter what the statistics say."

"Yes, I'm going to fight it. And I'm hoping I'll qualify for a clinical trial at the university. Have you heard about stem cell therapy?" I asked.

"Yes, a little. Are they using it to treat malignancy patients now?" she asked.

I launched into a lengthy explanation and after several minutes realized I was overdoing it. "Sorry, you didn't need to hear all that. I've been told I have a good chance of being accepted into the trial, but that's yet to be seen. If I am accepted, I may need to take a number of days off over the next several weeks. I'm sure HR will wonder why I'm taking so many personal days. I don't want to officially inform them of my diagnosis until I'm required to on Day 60. I'm afraid that if they discover I'm M-100 they'll be pushing me out the door sooner than I want to go. I'd like to hang on to my job as long as possible. I'm sure you understand."

"Of course. Let HR wonder as much as they want to. Even if they suspect something they can't do anything until you declare your 'M' status to them. If you get a pink slip before that, or if they try and pressure you in any way, just let me know. I'll handle it. So this stem cell therapy stuff sounds intriguing. When will you know if you're in?"

"Hopefully by Wednesday or Thursday of this week. I'm being fast tracked! It's nice to have connections," I said.

Julia paused before looking me in the eye and saying, "I have some connections, too. I'm going to be praying for you," she said.

"I'd appreciate that, Julia."

"Do you have any other options if you don't get into the trials?" she asked.

I told her about the plan to use medications and the Generator to strengthen my immune system. She sat there quietly for a minute and then said, "Dave, my brother lost his wife to malignancy and she went through a similar treatment plan. A few months after she died, my brother got a call from a lawyer, something about supposed problems with the Generator. They wanted to find out more about his wife's treatments. I don't know much more than that, but my brother got pretty angry at the lawyers trying to profit from his wife's death. He had a hard time believing what they said, but the more he looked into it, the more he wondered if they were right. Then he got really angry at the government and the medical establishment. After a while, he realized there wasn't anything else he could do, so he decided to let it go and get on with his life. I don't know much more about it, but I felt I needed to mention it to you. If you're interested, I can find out the name of the lawyer for you."

"I'm really sorry to hear about your sister-in-law. And I'm glad that your brother is learning how to live with it. I appreciate the offer to put me in touch with the lawyer, but don't worry, I've spent hours checking all this out. I think it's safe. It's not likely the Generator was responsible for your sister-in-law's death. Sure, I've encountered more than one group on the Net who claim it's dangerous, but hasn't that always been the case with new technology? My grandparents wouldn't use mobile phones, because they were afraid of getting brain cancer."

"Okay, I know how thorough you are. I trust your judgment," she said as she reached for the check.

"Oh no you don't," I said and tried to grab it.

"You don't have a chance. You know how stubborn I am," she said as she stood up.

"Thanks, Julia. I knew I should have ordered the steak sandwich," I said shaking my head. As we headed back to the office I wanted to tell her how much I appreciated and respected her, but all I could manage was, "You're a great boss, and I'm thankful to have worked for you for so many years."

She smiled and said, "Thanks. You and your people make me look good, Dave." We walked silently for a while and then she said, "If there's anything I can do, don't hesitate to ask. And I want you to keep me informed on how you're doing; my door is always open."

I knew she wasn't just saying that. She was genuinely concerned and that meant a lot to me. "Thanks so much. I'll be sure and keep you posted."

As I drove home that evening, Julia's words played over and over in my mind. I wondered if the law firm ever discovered any real problems or if it was just some sort of scam. I decided to do a little investigating.

After supper I spent some time on the Net and found out that there were health advocacy groups lobbying to have the Ministry of Health conduct additional testing of the Generator. They argued that there was a connection between malignancy and the Generator, but they couldn't prove it. I also found two law firms that were planning class action lawsuits against Future Health, claiming their clients contracted malignancy from exposure to the

Generator. I began to wonder whether it was as safe as it was purported to be. I decided to give Julia a call.

When she answered, I could see she had guests. "Hi, Julia. I see you're busy, so I won't keep you. If you have time in the next day or two, would you be able to find out the name of the lawyer you told me about at lunch?"

"Absolutely. I'll call my brother later tonight. I'll call or send you a message as soon as I find out."

"Thanks. See you tomorrow."

"Have a good evening, Dave."

As I sat there thinking, I began to feel unsettled. It reminded me of when I was a teenager and some friends and I swam into a dark cave and started exploring it. My impulse was to turn back and get out of there, but something compelled me to go a little farther to see what we might find. I wondered if I was on the verge of a similar experience.

Chapter 6

Day 90 – Tuesday, May 13th

Julia stopped by my office the next morning and gave me the name of the law firm the lawyer worked at. "Have you decided to talk to them?" she asked.

"I plan to call them during lunch."

"Why don't you call right away? And let me know what you find out, okay?"

After she left I called the law firm and spoke to three different people before they connected me to someone who was working on the Generator case. "Hello. My name is Maria Moreno. How can I help you?" she asked.

"My name is Dave Roberts. I'm not sure if you can help me or not, but I'm trying to find out if there are any risks involved with the Generator, and someone suggested I call your law firm."

"Do you have cancer?" she asked her voice sounding somewhat aloof.

"No, malignancy," I said and went on to tell her about my M-100 status and that I was considering treatment with the Generator.

"We are planning to file a class action suit in the near future. If you have any reason to believe the Generator is responsible for your malignancy, we would like to meet you," she said.

"To be a plaintiff?"

"Yes, if you qualify."

"I'll think about that. But I was hoping to get information about why you believe it is dangerous. Is there someone else I could contact about that? I start treatment in two days."

"Two days!" she said and there was a pause. "Can I call you later? I might be able to help you," she said sounding a little more sympathetic.

"Call me whenever you can and thanks," I said and disconnected.

I waited all day for her to call and started to wonder if she really would get back to me. "She's a lawyer; I'm sure she has a dozen things on her mind," I thought.

I was driving home when Hailey announced, "Call from Ms. Moreno. Connect?"

"Connect. Hello, Ms. Moreno."

"Hello, Mr. Roberts. I'm sorry to keep you waiting, but I had trouble reaching the person I needed to talk to. Can you meet me in an hour?" she asked.

"An hour! Yes, I probably can. It depends on where I guess. Is it that urgent?"

"We shouldn't waste any time. I was thinking of the Stone Hearth Coffeehouse."

Slightly surprised I said, "That's near my house."

"That's why I chose it. Can you be there at 6:30?"

"I'll be there."

"I'll be wearing a black and white business suit with a yellow scarf," she said.

As I disconnected, I suddenly had a mental picture of myself as a teenager about to enter into that dark cave.

I called Monika to explain why I would be late getting home. I arrived at the coffee shop ten minutes early and grabbed a muffin to hold me over until supper. As I walked toward a table I saw a woman coming through the door. She was dressed in a black and white business suit, and a yellow scarf, and looked to be in her mid-40s, with long black hair and brown eyes. I walked up to her and said, "Ms. Moreno?"

She greeted me with a warm smile and handshake, and said, "Please call me Maria."

"And you can call me Dave."

She bought a cup of tea and then we sat down at a corner table. She asked me what kind of work I did and if I had a family. I bragged on my kids for a couple of minutes and then asked about her family. She told me she was a widow and that her husband had died of malignancy three years ago. She explained that her brother was involved with an advocacy group that believed the Generator might be the cause of malignancy.

"He tried to warn me and my husband about the Generator, but we didn't believe him. Then when my husband died, I became convinced that my brother was on to something, and I asked him how I could help him. He asked if I would consider starting a class action lawsuit against Future Health, the manufacturer of the Generator. I persuaded my law firm to let me investigate the matter. For the last two years I've been trying to put together a case against Future Health. Our firm has interviewed nearly a hundred people who were infected with malignancy after being treated with the Generator. We've talked to others who lost loved ones who were treated with it. But we don't have any proof—yet," she said looking directly at me.

"So you don't really have any information to share with me," I said a bit frustrated and disappointed. "I thought you said you might be able to help me?"

"I want you to talk to someone else about this. He works for the advocacy group I mentioned. We all believe there is something wrong with the Generator, and I think you should be very careful. I understand that we've just met and you have no reason to trust me, but please believe me when I say that I'm not in this for personal gain. I lost my husband and I don't think he should have died. You have a family that needs you. Explore this a bit further—if not for yourself, then for their sake," she pleaded.

I wanted to get up and leave, but when she said, "explore this a bit further," I hesitated. I pictured myself exploring that cave again. "Why did she use that expression?" I thought.

"Does this other person have information that you don't?" I asked.

"If you mean does he have proof that the Generator is harmful, as a lawyer I'd have to say no. But three years ago if I had the information he has, I would never have allowed my husband to be treated with the Generator," Maria said.

"Alright. But why aren't you sharing that information with me now?"

"Honestly, I can't explain to you right now why it's important to meet with him. It will only take an hour or two more of your time. What do you say?"

I knew I had to take the next step. I was actually more than a little curious and even a bit excited in a strange way.

"When do you want me to meet him?" I asked.

She looked pleased and said, "I prearranged a meeting for tomorrow evening at 6:30 at Pleasant Oaks Park. If you didn't agree to the meeting, I was supposed to let him know. Come alone. You'll need to use public transportation. And you'll need to leave your mobile net device at home."

I was now apprehensive and somewhat suspicious. But I considered her conditions. She wanted a public meeting place with other people around, but where we could still have a private conversation. And she wanted me to be "off the grid," an expression I learned from Jaz which meant Guardian Security had no way to find me. If I drove my car or carried my MiNDi, they could locate me if they wanted to. But I didn't like being without my MiNDi.

"Can't I just power it off?" I asked.

"What model do you have?"

"The 9G."

"Leave it at home. Did you know that the newer models like yours keep their GPS chip activated even when they are powered down? Guardian Security can locate your MiNDi whenever they need to—or want to."

Monika probably knew that, but it was news to me. I wasn't too surprised though. I'm sure the government approved this "enhancement" in the name of national security. I decided to negotiate a condition of my own.

"I'll go through with it, but I want you to be there as well," I said firmly.

"Fair enough. I'll be there. You'd make a good lawyer, Dave," she said with a grin.

"Where exactly do we meet?" I asked.

"Just south of the pavilion there are some benches near the lake shore. You'll see a man wearing blue jeans and a black T-shirt that says 'Guardian Cares for You'."

"Good cover," I said.

She laughed and got up to leave.

Chapter 7

Day 89 – Wednesday, May 14th

The first thing I did in the morning was to check for messages. I was hoping to hear from Nucell, but the only message was from the clinic reminding me of my Thursday afternoon appointment.

My day at work passed slowly. I slipped out of the office a few minutes early, anxious to get to the meeting. I drove to the train station, parked, and remembered to leave my MiNDi in the car. After getting off the train, it was about a mile walk to the park. I arrived a few minutes early and saw my contact sitting alone on a bench. As I got closer I was a little surprised to see that he was so young—maybe in his mid-twenties. For some reason I was expecting someone a lot older. His hair was in a pony tail and reached to the middle of his back, and his beard was full, but neatly trimmed. He reminded me of myself when I was about 19 years old.

I walked up to him and said, "Hello. I'm Dave."

"You're early. I'm Kharis. Have a seat," he said motioning with his hand.

"Good to meet you, Harris," I said as we shook hands.

"That's Kharis. It's my moniker. It's from the Bible and means 'grace,' but you can call me Harris if you want to."

"So, are you a Christian?" I asked him.

"Yes, I am. What about you?"

"No."

"Have you considered it?"

"I've had some thoughts about God recently. I have lots of questions."

He stared out at the lake and said thoughtfully, "You know, so do I." Then he turned to look at me and said, "But I've found the answers to the important ones."

Right then I heard footsteps coming down the sidewalk and turned to see Maria approaching. "Good evening. Have you started yet?" she said.

"Just about to," said Kharis. He shifted his position on the bench, turning more toward me. "I'm part of a health advocacy group called 'Coalition Against Generator Exposure' or CAGE. The group is trying to alert people about the dangers of the Generator. We believe there is something wrong with it and that the Ministry of Health needs to launch an investigation. You may already know that Generator Prime was first put into use about 12 years ago, followed six years later by Generator Premier. Malignancy first started to appear about five years ago with the annual number of reported cases steadily increasing since then. That seems like a striking coincidence to us and to others as well. We've been trying to get the attention of the public, the medical community, and the Ministry of Health, but we haven't been very successful. You can understand some of the reasons why we've mostly been ignored. First, the Generator has been tested and approved by the Ministry of Health. Second, tens of thousands of people have been cured of cancer. And considering that millions of people have either been treated or screened by the Generator, the number of reported cases of malignancy is still proportionally very small."

"Yes, I'm aware that some people believe the Generator is somehow linked to malignancy. Maria told me that you have information that might convince me it is dangerous."

Kharis nodded, "I do, but I need to explain something to you first. Some of our activities are covert. I won't be able to answer all your questions about our organization and our operations. That's for our protection—and for yours."

"Covert. Is that a euphemism for illegal?" I asked.

"Yes," answered Kharis.

"But you said you're a Christian. Aren't you supposed to obey the laws?"

Maria answered, "We'd love to discuss ethics with you, Dave, but this isn't the time for that. I'll just say this: some of us believe that breaking the law is justified if it means lives will be saved. We are non-violent. Many in the group work as volunteers, serving totally at their own expense. Some put themselves at risk in order to help others. While there are members of our group who don't agree with our tactics—I'm referring to breaking the law—they are working hard in other ways for our cause. If you conscientiously object to what we do or how we do it, then we don't need to go any further. But please hear us out before you decide. One last thing: we expect you not to share this information with anyone else. Agreed?"

I wasn't expecting this. If had known I'd be meeting with a group that was involved in illegal activities, I probably wouldn't have come. I'm sure Maria knew that, and that's why she didn't give me those details. But I was here and curious to hear what they had to say. And who was I to say they were unethical or hypocrites? I thought about how many times I had bent the rules. It was easy to take an intellectual position on right and wrong; applying it consistently to one's own life was another matter. Besides, I bent the rules for my own benefit; they did it for the sake of others.

"I can't even tell my partner?" I asked.

"We'd prefer that you didn't say where the information came from," explained Maria.

"Okay, I understand. I'll listen," I said.

Kharis spoke again, "Good. About a year ago we gained Level 6 access to the NHD and acquired the records of everyone infected with malignancy. Every person diagnosed with malignancy was either screened or treated with the Generator. Do you understand? There are tens of thousands of cases of malignancy on file and they were all exposed to the Generator and then later diagnosed with malignancy."

Those statistics frightened me, and all of sudden their claim that exposure to the Generator and malignancy were related struck me as being more credible. I couldn't help but wonder if the Generator was the cause of my malignancy. If Kharis was telling the truth, and those numbers were correct, then I could understand why they believed that the Generator needed to be investigated. Still, I was far from convinced.

"I admit that those statistics are frightening. But the Generator has been used on millions and millions of people. If it causes malignancy, why have so few of them become infected? Shouldn't there be a lot more cases of it?" I argued.

Kharis nodded his head as if in agreement and said, "That's a good point. Over 20 million people have been exposed to the Generator. And thankfully only an extremely small percentage of them have been diagnosed with malignancy. But we are convinced that something is not right; the Generator, or maybe the formulas, or possibly both need further testing. People's lives are at stake—including yours."

"So is that why you wanted to meet me, to warn me in person not to go through with my treatments?" I asked.

"Not exactly. We want you to help us," Maria said.

"How?"

Maria, who had been sitting on the other side of Kharis came and sat next to me and said, "The statistical evidence alone isn't strong enough—not yet anyway. By the time it is strong enough for an official investigation to be launched, thousands more might die. We need hard evidence to try and prevent that from happening. If we can show that the Generator is not working properly, we would have a strong case. For more than a year now we've been trying to obtain some evidence. Kharis will explain how. Over two dozen cancer patients have cooperated with our investigation, but we didn't uncover any problems. You're the seventh malignancy case we've approached; the other six turned us down. We're hoping you'll help us."

"Tell me what you're asking me to do."

Kharis explained, "We have a device that can capture the output from the Generator. You simply attach it to your abdomen with medical tape before you go in for your session. The technician will not see it under your gown. We'll pick it up afterward and analyze the data to see if there were any anomalies during the session. That's about it."

"What does 'that's about it' mean?" I asked.

Kharis spoke in a quieter voice as he said, "If we find something wrong, we hope you'll be willing to gather more data. And if you're caught . . ."

I broke in, "If I'm caught what will happen?"

"We don't know; nobody has been caught yet. But I assure you that you won't be breaking the law," said Maria.

"And if you find something wrong, you want me to gather more data, which means another treatment with the Generator, right?"

Kharis hesitated and then said, "Yes."

I was bewildered. "That's asking a lot. If you find out the Generator is somehow malfunctioning and possibly harming me, how can you ask me to undergo further treatments?"

Maria answered, "Because you might be helping a lot of people. But that question is premature. What about helping us with the first step? Kharis brought the device. You can take it and record tomorrow's session."

I wasn't sure what to make of all of this. I knew I wasn't ready to decide on the spot. And I definitely needed to talk it over with Monika first.

"I'm not ready to decide. I need time to think it over and to talk to my partner about it. I'm sorry. I respect what you are doing, but I'm not sure how deeply I want to get involved. If I decide to help, I'll contact you."

"Okay. We didn't expect you to decide right away. We'd appreciated knowing what you decide one way or another. Please call me when you've made up your mind. We think Guardian Security is monitoring our activities, so don't say or write anything over the Net that could alert them. If you want to help us, just call and say that you are interested in being a plaintiff in the class action suit. If you can't help us, say you've decided not to participate in the suit," Maria said.

Kharis stood up. "Whatever you decide, Dave, I wish you well on the road ahead. I'm going to be praying for you. I have something I'd like to give you," he said and reached into his backpack. "It might help you find answers to some of those questions you have."

He handed me a book that said "Words of Life" on the cover.

"Is this a Bible?" I asked.

"Yes. Do you already have one?"

"No. I've never even held one before."

"I think it's best to start reading what's called the New Testament. Start with the book named 'John's Report' and see what you think. Ask God to help you understand and ask Him if what you're reading is really true. I believe He answers those kinds of prayers."

When Kharis said that, I remembered Monika's words a few days earlier about God answering certain kinds of prayers, and I recalled that I had asked God to help me to know if he really existed. Maybe this was a coincidence, but I couldn't help but wonder if God might be answering my prayer.

"I'll give it a try. Thanks, Kharis," I said trying to pronounce his name properly.

"I hope we meet again, Dave," Kharis said as he hoisted his backpack. We shook hands and then he and Maria walked off together. As I headed toward the train station I felt uneasy and anxious. I regretted contacting the law firm. I didn't want to have to deal with this. Dr. Steele was a caring and gifted doctor. He was doing his very best to help me and I trusted him. I wondered what he would think if I told him what I just learned. But I knew I couldn't. Then I tried to imagine Monika's response when I told her what Kharis told me. She would be skeptical and want more evidence that something was wrong with the Generator. We were a lot alike in that regard. But I was the one with malignancy and the one facing Generator treatments. Ultimately I had to decide what to do.

On the train I looked at the other passengers around me. I watched a little boy a few seats in front of me as he pulled his mother's hat down over her eyes, and then he laughed as she pretended she couldn't get it off. A thought came into my head, "What if I could keep that little boy from contracting malignancy?" As I continued watching him I said to myself, "If I knew I could do that, it might be an easier decision." But I didn't know that for sure. I didn't even understand what my risks were. I wanted more information, something that could help me decide.

My thoughts became a little clearer as I was driving home. I decided to stick with Dr. Steele's plan and go through with the first Generator treatment tomorrow afternoon. Without more concrete evidence, I wasn't ready to give up on what might be my only chance to extend my life. I also thought about Maria's and Kharis's appeal for help. This was an opportunity for me to do something that might benefit lots of people. And since I had already decided to go through with the treatment, why not help them out? Then once the data was analyzed, I would have additional information, which might help me figure out the next step. I thought about what might happen if I got caught, but I wasn't too afraid. I would be careful; nobody would suspect a thing. As I thought about how I would do it, I got excited and felt a little adrenaline rush. "The name's Bond, James Bond," I said out loud in my best British accent.

As soon as I got home I explained everything to Monika leaving out the part about the group's covert activities and how they obtained the statistical information. She listened without saying a word, but I could tell she was suspicious.

When I finished she said, "That information isn't even available to Dr. Steele. You need Level 5 or 6 access to the NHD to get it, and even if someone in their group has that degree of access, they aren't allowed to share that kind of private information with anyone else. So CAGE is either associated with an informant who is breaking the law, or they know someone who hacked into the NHD, or maybe they hacked into it themselves. Which is it?"

"They didn't say exactly. And you're right; they're involved in some illegal activities. But don't you believe their cause is just? You're in favor of similar tactics used by other protest groups," I argued.

"I didn't say I was opposed to what they are doing. As a matter of fact, if they're that convinced something is wrong with the Generator, I think their efforts should be applauded. I'm just offended that you didn't explain that part to me. Don't you trust me?"

"Of course I trust you. I was trying to protect you. If I get caught and the police or Guardian Security questions you, the less you know the better."

"Hmm. I appreciate your concern, but in the future I think I'd rather have you be less protective and more open. So what do you think? Do you want to help them out?"

"Yes, I'd like to help—at least take the first step and capture data for one session. If they find something is wrong with the Generator, then I don't know what I'll do next. But we don't need to decide that now. What do you think?"

"If you want to help them, I'm okay with it, but it makes me nervous."

I called Maria and told her I would like to participate in the class action suit. She said she would call me back in a few minutes. Within 20 minutes she called and said someone would meet me at my office in the morning to take my statement. She thanked me several times and told me there was nothing to be concerned about. She was probably right, but I was awake for several hours that night imagining just about every way something could go wrong."

Chapter 8

Day 88 – Thursday, May 15th

There was still no news from Nucell this morning. Dr. Steele told me I could expect to hear from them by Wednesday or Thursday, so I hoped they would contact me sometime today.

I arrived at work and was walking to the front entrance when I noticed Kharis sitting by the fountains. He saw me and stood up as I walked toward him.

"Nice place to work. What do you do?" he asked.

"Try and keep our customers happy," I said.

"Did they give you any samples of the latest Bio-chips? I'd like to get my hands on one."

"I've got one in here if you've got a scalpel on you," I said extending my left hand. He pulled out a pocket knife and started to open it. I quickly put my hand in my pocket. "It's really not the latest version just in case you have any ideas," I told him.

"Too bad, I'm pretty good with a blade," he said with a smile. Then he put the knife away, reached into his backpack, and took out a small leather case. He discretely opened it to show me the device, and then quickly closed it. "All you have to do is tape this to your abdomen. When the session is over, bring it to me. I'll be in the café on the corner, down the block from the clinic." He handed me the case and a small package of medical tape. "Do you have any questions?"

"No. I think I can handle it," I said with a hint of sarcasm.

"Your appointment is at 4:00, right?"

"Right. I should be done by 4:30 or so."

Kharis slung his backpack over his shoulder and looked me in the eye. "Dave, thanks so much for doing this. I wish I could tell you how much it means to us. I've been asking God to help us find the right person for a long time. I think you are his answer."

"Maybe we should wait to see how this turns out before you jump to that conclusion," I said and headed for the entrance. "See you later."

I had a tough time concentrating at work and didn't accomplish much in the morning. We had a departmental meeting after lunch, but I didn't feel like we made much progress, and it was mostly my fault. I turned the meeting over to one of my assistant managers and left the office around 3:15 for my appointment.

I got more and more nervous the closer I got to the clinic, and I nearly went through a red light. I checked in and had to wait about 20 minutes before the technician led me to the room where I would undress. I closed the door, changed into the hospital gown, and while standing in front of the door to prevent someone from walking in on me, I took out the device. It was about as big as a half of a piece of chewing gum, and after taping it to my stomach, it was imperceptible under the gown.

The treatment session took about 15 minutes including the imaging scan of my pancreas. When it was over I removed the device, put it in the case, and set it on the chair while I put my clothes on. I felt elated that it was over, and I was anxious to get to the café. I went out to talk to the receptionist about my next appointment when a voice behind me said, "Excuse me, did you just come from Imaging?"

I turned around and a woman was standing there. I could see she had something in her hand. I suddenly remembered I had left the case on the chair. I tried to stay calm and act nonchalant. It looked like the case was closed, and even if she had opened it to see what was inside, it was unlikely she had a clue as to what it was.

"Yes, I did."

"Did you forget something?" she asked showing me the case.

I felt panicky and hesitated a second or two before answering, "Yes, that's mine. Thanks so much. I'm glad you caught me before I left."

"You're welcome. Is it some kind of new Net device?"

She caught me off-guard. "No, no. Well, sort of. It's a prototype of . . . of an advanced Bio-chip that can connect to the Net without using a scanner. I work for UBC, Universal Bio-chip Corporation." I quickly took it from her hand and as I headed for the door said, "Thanks again. My boss would have been upset if I lost this."

"Kind of big for a Bio-chip," she said sounding a bit doubtful.

I turned to look at her.

"Ugh. I wouldn't want that implanted under my skin. I think I'll stick with the one I have," she said and smiled.

I smiled back and kept moving toward the door.

"Hey," she said raising her voice. I stopped, but didn't turn around. "Be more careful next time. Your job might be at stake."

"Trust me, it won't happen again," I said as I walked through the door. As I headed to the café I could feel my heart beating and thought, "What next time? I think my secret agent days are over."

A few minutes later as I retold the story to Kharis, I felt much better. The experience was exhilarating and I hadn't felt like that for a long time. He said he understood the feeling, and that he had had a couple of similar experiences.

"I'd like to hear some of those stories," I said to him.

He stood up and said, "I hope we can work out a time to have a talk. Right now I'm anxious to get this data analyzed. Thanks again for your help."

"How long until you'll have the results?" I asked as we exited the café.

"Possibly by Friday night, but more likely on Saturday. I'll be in touch."

"Thanks. I hope to see you again soon . . . I think. Well, you know what I mean," I said as we headed off in different directions.

I got home and Monika was sitting at the table waiting anxiously for me. I reported everything that happened, and when I got to the part about leaving the device on the chair, she was wide-eyed. She started laughing when I told her that I said to the woman, "It's a prototype of an advanced Bio-chip."

"You're kidding! Brilliant answer. Did she believe you?"

I laughed with her. "I'm not sure; she seemed doubtful. But I didn't stick around to discuss it."

"You never were very good under pressure. Anyhow, I'm glad it's over. When will you hear the results?"

"Friday night or Saturday. They'll contact me."

I was tired and went to bed early. Nucell had not contacted me, so I planned to call Dr. Steele the next day to see if he heard anything. I also wanted to find out the results of today's scan.

Chapter 9
Day 87 – Friday, May 16th

As soon as I woke up I asked Hailey if there were any new messages, but there weren't any. I was getting concerned. I went to work and waited until mid-morning before calling Dr. Steele hoping that he would have my scan results by then. The receptionist said he was with a patient and that he would call me back.

By the time I got back from lunch Dr. Steele had still not called. I tried to get some work done, but I wondered why it was taking so long for him to get back to me. It was almost 3:00 when he finally called.

"Hello, Dr. Steele. Are you having a busy day?"

"Hello, Dave. I apologize for the delay. I wanted to verify the results of yesterday's scan before calling you."

I didn't like the sound of that. If he wanted to verify the results, it probably meant bad news.

"Is there anything wrong?" I asked.

"I'm afraid so. Do you want to come in to discuss it?"

"I'm alone and I'd rather hear it now."

"The malignancy is still progressing at a faster than normal rate in the pancreas. It hasn't spread to any other organs, but the computer has lowered your 'M' rating by five days. That puts you at M-82. I know it sounds bad, but as I've said, it's possible that the spread of the infection will slow down. I've seen it happen, but we can't count on it."

I was stunned. "How? Why is it spreading so quickly? What can we do?"

"Hope that our approach will be effective. We'll have to wait until next week to see if the Generator treatment helped. The medications don't seem to be doing much yet, but they haven't had much time to work. I'm afraid I can't explain why it's spreading this quickly."

"Did Nucell contact you today?"

"No, so I called Brandon. He is out of the country and he didn't know why we haven't been notified yet. He thought we should hear something today. If for some reason we don't hear from them, he will look into it. He gets back tomorrow, but he won't know anything more until Monday. There's nothing else we can do for now. I'll call you as soon as I hear from Nucell."

"Okay, thanks. I'll try and keep my mind off of it, otherwise I'll just worry."

"Find something to distract yourself. Watch a movie or read a good book. Worrying won't change a thing. Easier said than done, I know."

"I'll do my best. Goodbye, doctor."

M-82! Five more days of my life gone and there was no explanation. And I was concerned that maybe Nucell would never process my application. I was upset and feeling depressed. I tried calling Monika. She didn't answer and I didn't leave a message. I walked over to Julia's office. She saw me and motioned for me to come in.

"Hi, Dave. Come in and sit down. Close the door if you want to."

I closed the door, but didn't sit down.

"Julia, I just spoke to my doctor. The malignancy is spreading faster than normal. I've been reclassified to M-82."

"Oh no! Dave, I'm sorry. Did he have any idea why it's spreading so fast?"

"No, they don't have any idea. I don't think anybody really understands much about this disease. Five years and where have they gotten finding a cure? And they don't seem to have a clue about what causes it."

"But you just started treatment. Isn't it too soon to know if it will help? Don't you need to give it more time?"

"I wish I had a little more time. Do you mind if I take the rest of the day off? I'd rather HR didn't know I'm taking time off again, although it probably doesn't matter anymore."

"Sure. I'll cover for you if they notice you've left. Go home and get some rest. And if you need more time off, let me know. I'll do what I can."

"Thanks, Julia. I'll be in on Monday."

When I got home, I changed clothes and went for a walk. But all I could think about was how hopeless things looked. I cut the walk short and returned home. I sat down to see what was on the news, but couldn't keep my mind on it. I thought about doing some work so I got my briefcase. When I opened it I saw the Bible Kharis gave me. I turned off the news, picked it up, and opened to the table of contents. Kharis told me to start with the New Testament, but I couldn't recall what else he said. Then I noticed an entry for "John's Report" and remembered that's what he suggested I read. I turned to it and read:

"In the beginning the Word already existed. The Word was with God, and the Word was God. He existed in the beginning with God."

I wasn't sure what that meant, so I followed Kharis's advice. I prayed silently, "God, I'd like to know if you're real. Help me to understand what I'm reading. And if it's true, please show me that somehow."

I kept reading and discovered that some parts were hard to figure out, but most of it was fairly easy to understand. But understanding it and believing it were two different things. I liked what I read, but wasn't sure if it was true or not.

Over an hour passed and I had nearly finished "John's Report," when I heard Monika come in. She walked into the living room and said, "Hi, Davey. How was your day? Did you hear from Nucell?"

"No. But I got the results of yesterday's scan. Sit down."

She sat down next to me and after hearing my report, gave me a big hug. "It's discouraging news. But I just know you're going to get into the stem cell trial. Don't give up hope. You haven't been turned down yet," she said trying to encourage me.

"I know. I felt terrible after I got the news. I need to at least wait until I hear from Nucell before I let myself sink into despair," I said with a small grin.

"Your sense of humor is still working fine I see. Is that a Bible you're reading? I've been meaning to get one of those. What made you go buy one?"

I had forgotten to mention how Kharis had given it to me.

"Kharis gave it to me. Did I tell you he's a Christian? Yes, I'm sure I did when you asked about his strange name. You should read it. There's some stuff that's a little hard to understand, but it's fascinating."

Monika picked it up and said, "I'll read what you just read and we can discuss it. Deal?"

"Then when do I get to read it? I guess I'm going to have to buy a digital copy after supper."

"You can read the book; you know I prefer to read on my DigiPad," Monika said getting up. "I'm famished; let's eat! I'll get supper ready."

"Sounds good. Then I can finish these last few pages. Are you offering to clean up, too?"

"Nice try. You know I'm not that easy."

Chapter 10
Day 81 – Saturday, May 17th

Jasmine called in the morning. I gave her the news and she cried. She had called to let me know she was doing her best to arrange time off of work, but she wouldn't be able to make it home until the end of the month. I was disappointed, but I was glad she was able to come at all. She asked if I read the articles she sent and what I thought about them. I had to confess that I hadn't started yet.

"I have the whole weekend free. I promise I'll spend some time reading them," I told her.

"Thanks, Dad. Will you get in touch with me as soon as you hear from Nucell?"

"I promise to call you as soon as I hear from them," I assured her.

———————————

Just before lunch Lori surprised us and showed up at the front door. When I told her about my new diagnosis, she looked like she wanted to cry, but didn't. She took after her mother, Anne, in that respect. Anne hated to cry in front of others. One of her goals in life was to make others happy. If she did feel sad or down, she wouldn't let on. Lori was a lot like that, but I could always see past her façade.

"Lori, having you here makes me feel so much better. I'm not afraid. And I might get accepted into the stem cell trial. I've been asking God to help me."

"Really? I didn't think you prayed or believed in a God. Has something changed? Wait, of course, it has. But do you think God really exists? I guess you do if you prayed to him. But nobody can know for sure. I suppose it's a good idea to pray, just in case He does exist. But why would . . . Oops, sorry, Dad. Caleb sometimes ignores me when I drone on and on. At least you always listen," Lori said looking into my eyes.

Monika smiled at us and said to Lori, "And do you know what else? We've been reading the Bible."

"Really? What's it like? I've heard there are lots of different Bibles. How did you know which one to get? Can you understand any of it? Don't you need to go to a school or . . ." She stopped and sighed. "Okay, maybe we should get lunch ready, Monika. Then I'll try and listen for once. It's easier to do that when I have food in my mouth."

Lori had to leave after lunch. I went to the study to read some of the articles Jasmine sent me. I browsed several of them and was amazed that there was so little research to back up most of the alternative remedies being discussed. Of course, there was virtually no funding available to conduct research into them, since it was so hard to make money in the natural medicine field. There were plenty of people claiming that they had been healed of malignancy and many other diseases, and I found their stories intriguing, but before I would be willing to give natural remedies a try, I wanted more definitive evidence that they were effective. Still, I noted down several topics that I wanted to explore further. And it would give me something to discuss with Jasmine when she came to visit.

After a couple of hours of reading the material Jasmine sent I took a break. I made myself a snack and sat down on the porch to read the Bible again. I had decided to start at the beginning of the New Testament. I liked to be methodical, and I decided to read the entire New Testament from the beginning to the end. "Matthew's

Report" was the first book in the New Testament. It told the story of Jesus' life just like "John's Report," but after reading a few chapters I could tell his writing style was quite different. It seemed to present a more orderly, historical account, and I found that appealing.

At supper Monika and I discussed the Bible. She had only read the first six chapters of "John's Report," but she had a lot to say. I listened to some of her insights and questions. I could answer a few of them because I had learned a few more things about Jesus' life by reading "Matthew's Report." She decided to read part of that book as well. That was just like her. She was usually reading four or five books at any given time. I can't imagine how she kept them all straight.

Chapter 11
Day 80 – Sunday, May 18th

Monika was still sleeping when I got out of bed. I decided to make breakfast for the two of us. I was in the mood for an omelet, and the smell of them cooking and the coffee brewing brought her into the kitchen.

"What a great way to be woken up! Thanks for making breakfast. You didn't put garlic in my omelet, did you?"

"Of course not. After all these years, I think I can remember something like that," I said.

As we ate, Monika surprised me by asking me if I had ever thought about getting married. We hadn't known each other very long before deciding to move in together. After living together for two months, I asked her if she wanted to sign a Domestic Partner Limited Agreement. We never really considered marriage.

She said, "I've been reading about marriage in the Bible. It's in lots of different places. I'm not saying I want to become a Christian yet, but it seems clear to me that God wants a man and a woman to make a lifetime commitment to each other. It's hard to explain, but it's like something inside of me is saying, 'Yes, that is the way it should be,' but at the same time I can think of lots of good reasons for not getting married. And we've gotten along just fine without it. Do you understand what I mean?"

"I understand the part about having an internal debate. I've been reading some of the teachings of Jesus and that's what I've experienced. On one level I agree with what he says, but on a different level my mind is protesting. Maybe I'm just trying to find excuses for my behavior, because I realize I'm not doing a very good job of living up to his standards."

"Neither am I. Being a Christian seems almost impossible."

"But attractive in a lot of ways. We were talking about marriage though," I said.

"Right. I never really understood why some people place so much value on getting married. I'd guess over half of our friends and co-workers aren't married. And some of them who were married have gone through a divorce—or two. So what's the advantage of getting married?"

"I can think of plenty of advantages—especially when children are involved. The thing that scares me is having to make a commitment to stay married for the rest of your life. That seems like a recipe for failure. Who knows what could happen after 10, 20 or 30 years? How can people promise to stay together that long?"

"I could, if it was with you," Monika answered.

Just then, thankfully, there was a knock on the front door. I glanced at the monitor and saw that it was Kharis. I got up quickly, went to the door, and opened it.

"Kharis! What a surprise. Come in. Why didn't you call? Do you have any news?" I asked and then remembered my manners. "I'm sorry. Come in and sit down. How about some breakfast?"

"No thanks. But I'll have some coffee. I didn't want to call; it could be risky. I have the results of the analysis and we think we've found what we've been looking for."

We sat at the table and Monika brought Kharis a cup of coffee. I was scared, but excited. "Tell us! Don't keep us in suspense."

"We converted the captured data into a Generator formula and compared it to all the formulas on public record. The formula that we recorded does not match any of those that have been registered with the Ministry of Health. So it appears that the Generator malfunctioned and now we have some hard evidence. You don't know how happy we are."

"But how could it malfunction? What about all the safety protocols?"

"We don't understand how it could happen. The Generator is a very sophisticated device and I imagine there are lots of ways something could go wrong. Did they design it to protect us from every possible anomaly? I can't say. That's way beyond our level of expertise."

I didn't want to ask the next question, but I had to know what they planned to do now. "You told me that if you found something amiss, that you would ask me to gather more data. Is that still the case?"

He stared into his coffee cup for a few seconds before he answered. "We have to be sure. We want to use two devices simultaneously next time. Then we can rule out the chance that the problem is with our device. And if we find something wrong again, we'll have a much better chance of getting somewhere with the Ministry of Health or Future Health. You can understand that, can't you?"

"Yes. If I was trying to prove the Generator wasn't working properly, I would do the same thing. But do you understand my position? How do I know that the Generator isn't harming me? What do you think? What are the chances that it gave me malignancy or that it caused it to spread more rapidly?"

As I said that I realized I hadn't told Kharis that I had been reclassified as M-82. I explained it to him and when I finished, he sat there silently.

Finally he said, "I wish I knew what to say. It's discouraging and it makes me angry. How are you handling it?"

"I was depressed for a while, but I've still got hope. I'm not ready to give up."

"Good. It's far from over. Have you heard yet if you got into the clinical trial?"

"No. I should have heard by now. My doctor put in a call and I think I'll hear something tomorrow."

"I'll be praying for you, Dave."

"I'd appreciate that," I said.

"I called our computer security expert this morning. He's been waiting a long time for this kind of breakthrough and he's excited to meet you. He plans to fly in from the west coast on Tuesday or Wednesday. Your next session is still scheduled for Thursday afternoon, right?"

"Yes. But why does he need to meet me?"

"I'm not sure. He more or less started CAGE almost five years ago and he probably wants to be personally involved now that we have some real evidence to work with. Or he might have some additional information that you should know. I think you should meet with him before your next session, but don't let him pressure you into a decision."

"It won't hurt to talk to him," I said.

"Good. I'm going to try to be there, too, but it would save me some time if I could leave the devices with you today. If you decide not to go through with it, I'll come pick them up."

"That's fine; go ahead and leave them. So what do you think? Do you have an opinion on how risky this is to me?"

"I think it's risky, but I have no way of determining how risky it is. If you decide to stop your Generator treatments, I'll understand. But when you're thinking this over, I hope you'll consider the other people you might be helping."

"That's what I'm doing. And I'm pretty sure I want to go through with it. But I want to wait a couple of days before making a final decision."

I wanted to change the subject and talk to Kharis about religion. As I sat there thinking about how to bring it up, Monika jumped in. "Kharis, thanks so much for giving Dave that Bible. We've both been reading it and it's got us thinking. Being a Christian looks so hard. I don't ever think I could do what Jesus asks us to do."

That was just like Monika. Just say what's on your mind and don't waste any time getting to the point. But I was glad she brought it up.

"You're right. In our own strength it's impossible. I failed miserably. But the Bible says everyone has failed; we've all sinned and no one has ever lived up to God's standards. That's why we need God's grace and mercy. Without it none of us have got a chance," Kharis said.

"So how did you decide to become a Christian?" Monika asked.

Kharis smiled and seemed more relaxed. ""I was hoping you'd ask me that," he said. "I grew up attending a denominational church. I started spending a lot of time with a girl when I was 15 and she changed my mind about religion. She thought it was a waste of time. Not long after meeting her, I stopped going to church. My parents were pretty upset about it, but they realized that making me go to church wasn't the solution, so they reluctantly gave in and let me have my way. Over the next few years I lived more and more for my own pleasures and thrills. I was quite a computer geek, and when I started at the university I met some guys who were into serious hacking. I was learning a lot from them, but then Guardian Security tracked them down, and they were kicked out of school and prosecuted. I'm not sure what happened to them, but that scared me away from hacking and back to my studies!"

He continued, "Around that time a high school friend of mine overdosed and died. I attended her funeral and her brother, Jason, got up to speak. He shared how he had recently come to faith in Jesus and explained the gospel. It seemed like the first time I had heard it, even though I attended church for all those years."

"So they didn't teach from the Bible in your church?" I asked.

"They did, and I'm not sure why it never resonated with me. I think there was lots of truth being taught, but not much grace. The ministers taught that we were supposed to obey God's word, but they didn't seem to have much joy in their lives. That was true of my parents, too. They attended church faithfully, and they knew the Bible pretty well. They did their best I guess, but looking back I don't recall seeing much evidence of grace in their lives. God's joy was definitely in short supply."

"What's the gospel?" Monika asked.

"The word means 'good news.' The good news is that even though we are all sinners and that there's no way for us to ever be good enough to get to heaven, God loves us and gave His son, Jesus, to pay the penalty for our sin. There's absolutely nothing we can do to earn God's love or forgiveness; it's a free gift. In the book of Ephesians, it says, 'God saved you by his grace when you believed. And you can't take credit for this; it is a gift from God. Salvation is not a reward for the good things we have done, so none of us can boast about it.'"

"But there must be something we have to do. Are you saying God automatically saves everyone?" Monika asked.

"No. I'm saying it's a gift; a gift needs to be received. And the way we receive it is to trust Jesus completely. In the book of

Romans it says, 'If you confess with your mouth that Jesus is Lord and believe in your heart that God raised him from the dead, you will be saved.' But there is a little more that you need to understand."

"I knew it must be more complicated than that," I said.

"It's not complicated, but it's costly," Kharis said.

"I thought you said it was free," Monika said.

"I'm not trying to confuse you. The gospel message is simple, and salvation is a free gift. But believing that Jesus died and rose from the dead is not just a matter of acknowledging some theological truth. It's important to understand that if you really believe in Jesus, you will accept his words, his teachings. He tells us that we must obey and follow him. That's what it means to confess, 'Jesus is Lord.' He must be the Lord over every area of our lives. The cost is giving up the right to control your own life and putting God in charge of it."

"Did you make that decision right away?" I asked.

"When I heard Jason's explanation at the funeral, I finally understood God's plan of salvation. Maybe I had heard it before, but this was the first time it impacted me. I knew it was true, but I didn't act on it right away. I went back to school and thought some more about it. I couldn't sleep that night, and as I laid in bed thinking, I decided I was tired of living life my way. I saw how sinful and selfish I really was and that inside I was full of fears and insecurities. I really didn't know what life was all about, and I was ready to give God a chance to show me. I asked Jesus to forgive me for all my sinful behavior and told him that I needed him in my life. Then it's hard to explain what I experienced. It felt like perfect love filled me up inside. The feeling lasted for quite a while and I just basked in it. I knew then that God had forgiven me and accepted me. I can't say how I knew, but I did—and I still do."

"So that's how a person becomes a Christian?" Monika asked.

"That's how it happened for me. Don't expect it to be that way for you. Everyone has their own story of how they came to faith in Christ. My brother's story is very different. For him it happened gradually over a period of several weeks. He couldn't tell you what day or even what week he became a Christian."

"But what about the verse you shared a minute ago. I get the part about making Jesus Lord of my life. That's a choice, right? But that part about believing in my heart . . . how do I do that? Is that a choice, too?" Monika said.

"That's not an easy question for me to answer. You can't just pretend to believe. And I think it's important that you don't try and fake it. My advice is to talk to God about it. Ask him to show you what faith is and how to really believe. The Bible says that if we seek him earnestly, we will find him. He's not trying to hide from us. In fact, the Bible teaches just the opposite: he wants us to find him, to know him and, best of all, to enjoy him. That last part is something I can't remember hearing about in church or seeing demonstrated in my parents' lives. And experiencing his joy is what makes it all worthwhile."

"I'm going to keep reading—and asking God to help me know the truth. I understand what you said, but I'm not sure if I'll ever get to the point where I really believe and don't have doubts and questions," Monika said.

"Like I shared with Dave, I still have lots of questions and I do struggle with doubts at times. But I have the answers to the important questions, and I no longer doubt God's existence or his love for me. That's a settled issue. But let him settle it for you in his own way. Just ask him to do it."

"I don't know what it will take to convince me, but I'm going to give it a serious effort," I said.

"I'm glad to hear that," Kharis said. "Now I better get going. I'm meeting Maria, and the buses don't run as frequently on Sunday."

I walked Kharis out to the porch and saw him off. "I'll be talking to you soon to let you know my decision about helping CAGE," I said.

"I'll be praying for you, Dave. Enjoy your afternoon. See you."

Chapter 12
Day 79 – Monday, May 19th

I no sooner got to work Monday morning and sat down at my desk when Julia poked her head in my office.

"Good morning, Dave. Did you have a good weekend?"

"Better than I expected," I said enthusiastically.

"I'm so glad. Does that mean you heard good news about the stem cell trial?"

"No, I haven't heard a thing yet. Hopefully I will today."

"Oh," she said. She stood there silently for a few seconds and then said, "Okay. Well, when you hear something will you let me know?"

"Absolutely."

"Thanks," she said and continued down the hall.

I got to work on the plans to reorganize our customer service operations. The morning was nearly gone by the time Dr. Steele called.

"Good morning, Dr. Steele."

"Good morning, Dave."

"Hold on one minute," I said and got up to close my door, then sat down again. "Have you heard from Nucell?"

"Brandon called. He checked to see what the status of your application was and gave me the update. They were behind a couple days and hadn't processed it yet. On Friday they were notified of your M-82 reclassification, so they made a special effort to discuss it and decide if it was too late to perform stem cell therapy and still get good results. Naturally they are trying to maximize their chances of success. They decided to accept you, but they want to place you in a control group."

"What does that mean?"

"It means that you will be put in a group with stricter conditions. In this case you must agree to not receive any Generator exposure for the entire four weeks you are in the trial."

"What do you recommend?"

"That you accept their offer and get in right away. It's the most promising option by far."

"That sounds good to me. When would I be able to start?"

"Thursday, May 29th."

"That's next week. I thought it would take longer to get in."

"That was my understanding as well, but since you are M-82 the situation has changed. They have sped up the process. If you're ready to say 'yes,' I'll call them right away. Do you need to talk to Monika first?"

"No, we've already discussed it. Please call them and let them know I'm ready. What's the next step?"

"I'll find out what I can when I talk to them. I'll either call or send you a message to let you know what they say. For now you need to stick to your treatment program. I see you've got your next Generator session scheduled for Thursday morning. I should have the results by that evening. Then we'll have a better idea if the immune boosting protocol is having any positive effect."

"Do you need to see me this week?"

"No, but maybe next week. I'll let you know."

"Thanks so much for all you've done. I'm feeling much more hopeful. I can't wait to tell Monika."

"You have a good reason to celebrate. I'll be in touch."

As soon as I finished the call with Dr. Steele, I tried to reach Monika, but she didn't answer, so I left a message to let her know that I was accepted into the clinical trial.

I sat back in my chair and closed my eyes, processing what just happened. I felt wonderful. I daydreamed about the days ahead. I thought about seeing Jasmine soon, and wondered if the three of us could get away to the lake for a couple of days. Then I thought about Monika and I taking a trip to visit her this summer. Maybe Lori and Caleb would be able to join us. We could all stay at a lodge in the mountains and have a great time. I thought of our last vacation in the mountains and the places I wanted to see again. Then a thought came into my head, "I might still die." Getting into the trial had filled me with renewed hope, but the fact was I didn't know what the outcome would be. It was okay to have some dreams, but I needed to be ready for the worst. I leaned over my desk and looked at my calendar. I had a meeting in 45 minutes and I wasn't ready. It was like splashing cold water on my face. "Nothing like a looming work deadline to bring a person back to reality," I thought.

Monika called and left a message while I was in the meeting. I called her back and she was beside herself with joy.

"It's wonderful! I kept saying you would get in, but inside I had my doubts. Now I have real hope again. Let's celebrate. How about our favorite Italian place tonight?"

"That sounds really good. I'll pick you up at the clinic. How does 6:00 sound?"

"I'll be ready. Have you called the kids yet?"

"No. I haven't had time. Let's call them together after I pick you up."

"Alright. I can't wait. See you soon. Ciao."

"Ciao."

I got to the clinic at 6:00 sharp and Monica was waiting for me. We called the kids from the car and told them the good news. They were both thrilled. When I explained to Jasmine about being in a control group that wouldn't allow me to undergo any more Generator treatments, she was really happy. It didn't have the heart to tell her that I would have another session or two before starting the trial.

I was too excited to sleep that night. I got up and went to the living room and picked up the Bible. I wanted to read the passages

Kharis had shared with us on Sunday. I was reading "The Letter to the Ephesian Church," chapter two, verses eight and nine where it says God saved us by His grace. For some reason I kept reading. Verse ten said, "For we are God's masterpiece. He has created us anew in Christ Jesus, so we can do the good things he planned for us long ago." I stopped. I read that last sentence over again. "He has created us anew in Christ Jesus, so we can do the good things he planned for us long ago." It seemed like God was speaking those words right to me! For the first time, I didn't have the impression that I was reading a historical account or someone else's mail. The words seemed personal. I read it again and then a fourth time. The words, "so we can do the good things he planned for us long ago," echoed in my mind. God was telling me that he had a plan for my life. I just sat there quietly with my eyes closed. Then I felt something I had never felt before. My insides were flooded with an indescribable sense of peace. That deep, nagging sense of worry and fear that seemed ever present in some secret chamber of my mind was completely gone. I relished the feeling for some time. Then my thoughts turned to God again. "You're real, aren't you?" I no longer doubted his existence or his love for me.

It was late when I finally went to bed. Monika was asleep. I wanted to wake her to share my experience with her, but then I thought, "No, I should wait." I still had that sense of peace. There was also a feeling of excitement, but it was a different kind of excitement than I had ever felt before. I was anxious to tell her what happened, but told myself there was a right time and place to do that. "God, help me to know how to share this with her," I thought as I drifted off to sleep.

Chapter 13
Day 78 – Tuesday, May 20th

"Hey! Are you going to get up today?" Monika was standing at the foot of the bed pulling my toes. I opened my eyes and looked at the clock. I had overslept. I got up quickly and Monika said, "I couldn't bring myself to wake you up earlier. You needed the sleep. Don't worry; you'll make it to work on time. There's coffee made and some oatmeal on the stove. I have to get going. See you tonight."

I got to the office at exactly 8:00 and got to work. Dr. Steele called me just after 9:00.

"Good morning, Dave."

"Good morning, Dr. Steele."

"I talked to Brandon and he put me through to the person in charge of your case. He gave me some basic information. You'll need to schedule an appointment at University Hospital by this Saturday for some tests. If those go okay, then the first stem cell transplant would take place the following Thursday. Over the four week trial there will be three or four transplants. Once the transplants are completed there will be several follow-up exams required during the first six months. I'll still be your primary care doctor and will probably need to see you at least twice during the first four weeks. They will send you a packet of information by tomorrow. How does that sound?"

"I still can't believe it! This is an answer to prayer. Please tell your friend Brandon how much I appreciate his help. I'd like to thank him personally as well."

"I can send you his Net address and number and you can contact him. That's it for now. Congratulations, Dave."

"Thanks. And thanks for everything you've done. I'll talk to you soon."

The rest of the morning passed quickly. I decided to eat my lunch out by the fountains. I picked up something from the cafeteria and went outside. It looked like half of the building had the same idea. It was a warm, sunny day in mid-May and it felt wonderful to be out in the fresh air. I wanted to find a more private spot to eat so I started walking down the street. In just a couple of minutes I was away from the crowd and in a quiet residential area. I couldn't believe how many flower gardens there were. They were amazing to look at. The lilac bushes were in bloom and the fragrance was intoxicating. "Why haven't I done this before?" I asked myself. As I walked and took it all in, my senses seemed keener than they had ever been. I couldn't remember when I felt so alive, and I hoped that feeling would never stop. It was one of the most enjoyable lunch hours I could remember.

Late in the afternoon Monika called to let me know that she had to work late. I decided to put in a couple of extra hours at the office as well. Around 5:15 Julia stopped by my office.

"Working late tonight?" she asked.

"Come in, Julia. Yes. Monika will be at the clinic until 7:30 tonight, so it's a good time for me to catch up on a few things."

"Dave, you don't need to worry about work. You have more important things going on right now."

I suddenly realized I hadn't told her about getting accepted into the trial.

"Julia, I found out yesterday that I've been accepted into the stem cell trial. I still have to pass some tests, but Dr. Steele doesn't foresee any problems. I'm sorry I didn't tell you, but I was so excited I just forgot. Forgive me."

Julia laughed, "Dave, don't worry about it. I'm so happy for you. So when do you start, and what does a stem cell trial involve?"

"If I pass the tests the first transplant will be next Thursday. The trial lasts four weeks and they said I'd likely receive three or four transplants. I'll have to take some time off, but not nearly as much as I expected."

"Four weeks. That seems quick to me. When do they expect to see results?"

"I don't know, but from what I've learned in my research, there is often noticeable progress within the first week after the initial transplant."

"So it's possible you're 'M' rating could change for the better in the next couple of weeks?"

"It's possible. I'm hoping that I won't ever reach M-60. Otherwise, that will be the end of my career with UBC."

"Not necessarily. This whole reporting process for 'M' status is still relatively new and I wouldn't despair yet. There are plenty of civil liberty groups saying it's discrimination and their lawyers are hard at work trying to get the law changed. But let's worry about all of that later. This is worth celebrating. Can I buy you lunch tomorrow?"

"That would be great. Thanks, Julia."

"Stop by my office at noon. And don't work too late."

"I'll try not to. See you tomorrow."

Chapter 14
Day 77 – Wednesday, May 21st

The next morning there was a message from Nucell and one from a Dr. Wells. Nucell sent me a document with some information about the trial. They reminded me to schedule an appointment at the hospital and in big red letters it said I would be rejected if the preliminary exam was not completed by Saturday. Under that was another red letter warning that said I would be rejected if any of the tests came back positive. A little further down the page was a similar warning saying I would be released from the trial if I had any Generator exposure during the four week period. Another warning stated that I would be expected to report to University Hospital by 10:00 a.m. on Thursday, May 27th.

They had my attention.

"Hailey, connect me to University Hospital."

I made my appointment for Saturday morning.

"Hailey, connect me to Human Resources at Universal Bio-chip Corporation."

I scheduled the morning off the following Thursday and then breathed a little easier. I opened the message from Dr. Wells and read, "Congratulations on being accepted into Nucell's Phase 2 Stem Cell Therapy Clinical Trial," and then noticed the same red letter warnings all over again. I sighed and stuffed the letter in my briefcase to read later.

I got in the car and headed for work. As I drove, I told God how thankful I was. I couldn't honestly say that being accepted into the stem cell trial was his doing or not, but I was feeling happy and grateful, and I wanted to share that with him. As I did, the image of that little boy and his mother on the train suddenly popped into my head. That sobered me up somewhat. I remembered what I said to myself on the train, "What if I could prevent this boy from contracting malignancy?" As I thought about this malicious disease, I experienced a slight feeling of anger. "How many others might suffer? And I have a small opportunity to make a difference." I wanted to help. The rational part of me started to protest and said I needed to think this through more carefully, but the intuitive part of my brain was in control this morning. I called Monika and told her what I was thinking.

"You aren't usually so impulsive. Don't you want to take a little more time to consider it? You don't need to decide this moment, do you?" she argued.

"I wouldn't call it impulsive. I've been mulling this over for several days. I want to go with my gut on this. All I can say is that it feels right," I countered.

"Then I won't try and talk you out of it. I've made lots of decisions based solely on intuition. Who am I to tell you it's the wrong approach? Besides, it's a selfless thing to do, and I admire you for it."

"It's settled then. I'll call Maria and let her know before I chicken out. I'll talk to you later. Bye, honey."

"Bye, Dave."

I called Maria and gave her the news. She was elated and thanked me several times. She told me that if everything went as expected, they would be read to present the evidence to the Ministry of Health and Future Health by next week. I was curious to see how this would all play out.

When I arrived at the office and was walking toward the entrance, there was Kharis sitting by the fountains again.

"Hi, Dave."

"Good morning, Kharis. What brings you here?"

"Proxy is in town and wants to talk to you. Can you meet him today?"

"Who's Proxy?" I asked.

"He's the computer security expert I told you about. I guess I never mentioned his name. His real name is Max, but everyone calls him Proxy."

"Great name. I get off of work at 5:00; I can meet you after that."

"How about the coffeehouse at 6:30?"

"Okay. How will I know him?"

"He has your description, but he's pretty easy to find. He's six foot three, weighs about 275 pounds, and is bald. If there's more than one person fitting that description in the place, he'll be the one with the gold stitching in his ear."

"Cool!" I said trying to sound like I met people like that on a regular basis. "Kharis, I've made up my mind to go through with it tomorrow."

"That's great! Thanks, Dave. I'm relieved, but not surprised. I plan to be at the meeting tonight so I'll see you then. Remember no MiNDi and use public transportation," he reminded me.

"Does a bicycle work?" I asked.

"Cool," he replied and started to leave. Then he turned and said, "Unless it's one of those recumbent jobs. Ugh!"

At 11:00 Julia stopped by my office. "Good morning, Dave. How's your day going?"

"It's been a good day so far. Are we still on for lunch?" I asked.

"I wanted to ask you if we can postpone our lunch plans. There are some issues with the new Bio-chip, and I have a conference call scheduled today during lunch to discuss our public response."

"Of course. I hadn't heard about problems with the Bio-chip. Is there anything I should know?"

"Just a minor glitch from what I've been told. We'll be putting out a company-wide memo in a day or two. Until then, don't mention it to anyone. And thanks for being flexible."

"Sure. Not a problem. Let me know when you want to reschedule."

"It may have to wait until next week. I'll get in touch with you about it later."

"Okay. Sounds good."

"Have a good afternoon, Dave."

It was a warm evening and I enjoyed a leisurely ride to the coffeehouse. As I was locking my bike I checked on the outdoor tables. They were all full, but nobody fitting Proxy's description was around. Inside it was pretty empty and I saw a big guy sitting in a booth by the front window; the gold thread in his left ear was shining from the sunlight coming through the window. I walked up and he looked me over.

"I hope you're going to take that silly looking helmet off. You might draw attention to yourself," he said dead seriously. Then he stood up and a couple of people outside looked through the window and stared at him. He turned his head to look at them, then turned to look at me again and said, "See I told you. Better take it off." We shook hands and he squeezed so hard I grimaced.

"Might as well get yourself something to drink before we sit down. Kharis will be joining us, but I can fill you in before he gets here," he said.

I went to the counter and bought a cold drink and then came back to sit down. "Did you fly in from the coast just to talk to me?" I asked.

"Yup. You're the key to putting a stop to this craziness. People are dying, families are suffering, and the government and big corporations could care less. It's all about money. I know, I know—Kharis probably warned you that I can easily get carried away and start ranting about how downtrodden we little people are, but don't worry I've got more important things on my mind right now. We've got a chance to make this thing work, but I want to be realistic. Maria thinks we can put together a strong case with a little more evidence, but the Goliath that we're facing is much bigger than you can imagine. Taking on the Ministry of Health or a mega-corporation like Future Health is almost lunacy for a group like CAGE with its limited resources. If they won't listen to us this time, I think our best shot is to go to the press. I'm sure they'll be willing to hear us out this time, if we tell them we have proof that the Generator is malfunctioning. If we can work with the press to arouse the public, then they will pressure the government to launch an investigation."

"You're probably right. But I'll leave that up to you and to CAGE. How long have you been with them?"

"Five years. But I'm not on staff; I'm a volunteer and help them with their computer systems and security when I can. My wife and I have a small business as Net security consultants: 'Max and Rose Net Control – When it comes to digital security, you must be serious.'"

"Malignancy only started to appear about five years ago. Did you assume there was a connection between the Generator and malignancy right away?"

"I was suspicious right away. Over eight years ago when I was still working for Guardian Security there was a cyber attack on Future Health's computers. They stole all the R&D records for the Generator formulas. We saw the attack and tried to trace it, but back then Net security wasn't developed to the degree it is today. We never caught the guy. Within a few weeks some of those records were published on the Net. Guardian Security shut down the site within 48 hours, but a few weeks later they were published on another site hosted in another country."

"I've read about similar cases, but I don't remember anything about this one."

"It didn't make a very big impact and hardly got any media coverage. Future Health was able to diffuse the situation, and it faded from the news quickly. But what I learned scared me."

"And what was that?"

"Future Health tested thousands of formulas in their quest to find a cure for cancer and other diseases. Most of the formulas were innocuous; they seemingly had no ill effects at all. But other formulas had clearly negative results. Some caused cancer cells to reproduce more quickly; others caused damage to healthy cells—

sometimes latent damage and sometimes almost immediate damage. So when malignancy first appeared, I couldn't help but wonder if the Generator had something to do with it."

"Yes, in my research into the Generator I ran across references to those findings. But it didn't strike me as too surprising. It's certainly not unusual in medical research to accidentally discover something that turns out to be harmful instead of helpful."

"No. That's to be expected. And things can go wrong. Just look at all the examples of medical devices that had to be recalled because they didn't perform as expected, or prescription drugs that were taken off the market because they had dangerous side-effects. And that's my point; I think they need to pull the plug on the Generator until they can fix what's wrong with it."

"I'm willing to help. I've discussed this with Kharis and unless there's some new information I need to know, I'm ready to go through with the data capture tomorrow."

"I was hoping you'd say that. Kharis was confident you were the man for the job."

"I still don't understand why you wanted to meet with me."

"I think we need to dig a little deeper and I'm here to discuss it with you."

Just then Kharis came in and joined us. After a few handshakes and hellos, Kharis asked what he missed.

"I've mainly been telling Dave what he already knew— stalling until you decided to join us. You're late."

"Don't mind him, Dave. He's usually pretty cranky. Are you in some kind of rush Proxy?" Kharis asked.

Proxy ignored that question and said, "I just told Dave that I want to take a few more steps and investigate this a little further."

"What for? Won't the data prove there's a problem with the Generator?" Kharis asked.

Proxy answered, "Yes, it will. But you know how long it can take to go through all that bureaucratic red tape before any action is taken. If we have additional evidence, we might be able speed that process up. Besides, I'm curious and want to see if we can determine what went wrong."

"What do you suggest?" Kharis asked.

Proxy replied, "Dave is, or rather has the key, to our next step."

Kharis said, "I don't follow."

"You probably know most of this, Kharis, but I want Dave to understand as well. Do you know how the Generator works, Dave?"

"Just the basics. My doctor explained how the formulas are put together and told me about the different variables, and so on, but I don't know much more than that."

Proxy continued, "That's helpful; I'll start from that point. Currently, there are 92 formulas registered with the Ministry of Health. When your doctor determines which formula to use for your Generator session, he just enters a code, let's suppose it's G-87, into your health record in the NHD. When you show up for your session you scan-in, the computer accesses your health record in the NHD, sees that you need formula G-87, and then tells the Generator to load that formula. The Generator only allows one formula at a time to be loaded, and once the session is finished it automatically clears it from memory. Those are basic safety protocols. After the Generator loads the formula the technician verifies everything and then just pushes the 'Start' button."

"Simple enough," I said.

"What I want to do at your session tomorrow is verify the formula the Generator runs. I've already figured out how to get to the Generator on the Net, but I haven't been able to break through to the part where the formulas are stored—the security system is too strong. It's like a heavily locked door, and to top it off the locks are changed on a regular basis. But you have a key!"

"What key?" I asked.

"It's right there in your left hand," Proxy said.

"Do you mean my Bio-chip?"

"That's right. When you scan-in, the computer has a key—your key—which opens the door to the Generator. During the brief time the computer communicates with the Generator, I can essentially watch what the Generator is doing. So when the Generator loads the formula, I'll be able to make a copy of it on my computer."

"I'm not sure I understand how all this works, but I don't need to, do I?"

"Not at all. The point is that during your session I'll be able to record a copy of the formula the Generator is using on you. Once I have a copy of the formula I can compare it to the formulas registered with the Ministry of Health, just like I did with the data we captured. If for some reason it doesn't match any of the registered formulas, then we know the problem is with the formula. If we find out the formula is fine, then we've eliminated it as a potential problem. But I think there's a good chance that something is happening to the formula."

Kharis interjected, "Maybe something is happening to the formula, but it could just as easily be a hardware issue. The problem could be a design flaw or a batch of defective microchips."

"You could be right, but I have no way to check the hardware. However, I can check the formulas—at least one of them. And besides, I have a hunch," Proxy said and paused.

"Are you going to let us in on it?" Kharis asked.

"Not right now. Let's see what happens tomorrow before I say anymore."

"Does any of this change what I need to do?" I asked.

"No. You do exactly what you did last time, except with two devices. I'll take care of the rest. I just need to make a copy of your key," Proxy said and took out a miniature scanner. "Hold out your hand."

He scanned my Bio-chip and then put the scanner back in his pocket and said, "What time is your appointment?"

"Four o'clock."

"Just before they call you in for your Generator session, I want you to send a message to this Net address. It will notify me that I need to start my monitoring program. I need to limit the time I communicate with the clinic's computer system. The longer I'm connected, the more likely it is I could be discovered. But I should be able to cover my tracks fairly easily for a short period of time."

"I'll be glad when this is over. I sure hope it pays off. There's going to be a huge public outcry if it turns out the Generator is causing malignancy," I said.

"We're counting on it. That's often what it takes to get something done. You'll be a hero, Dave," Kharis said.

I was stunned. That idea never crossed my mind before that moment. I didn't want any credit; CAGE was the one that did all the work. "Stop right there," I said. "I don't want to be connected to this in any way. If I can't remain anonymous, then I won't let you use my data."

Proxy and Kharis stared at me. Proxy spoke to Kharis, "I'm sure Dave has his reasons for taking that position. What will it do to our legal case if we refuse to identify the person who collected the data?"

"I'll have to talk to Maria about that, but I don't think it will matter. If we ever do get to trial, he may need to be identified to the court. But I really don't think we'll have to go that far. Regardless, we aren't going to identify you to anyone without your permission, Dave. I promise you."

"That's good enough for me," I said. "Are we done?"

"That's all I have," Proxy said.

"Proxy, when will you have some information for us?" Kharis asked.

"Tomorrow evening. I think we should plan to meet here again at 8:00 tomorrow night."

"I'll be here," Kharis said.

"I'll plan on it as well," I said.

Chapter 15
Day 76 – Thursday, May 22nd

I got to the office early Thursday morning to try and catch up on my work, but my mind kept wandering. Now that I was only hours away from my appointment—and another scan—I was questioning my decision. I had been doubtful of the connection between malignancy and the Generator, but the more I considered it, the more I was becoming convinced that it could be true. After my last scan my malignancy mysteriously spread at a faster than normal rate. I know Dr. Steele said that the rate of spreading can speed up, or slow down, but he offered no explanation for why that might happen. If the scan was to blame, then what would another session do to me? I tried to look at it objectively. Even if it did cause a slight increase in the number of malignant cells, I would start stem cell therapy in a week. The risk didn't seem too great. And I might be helping thousands of people. But no matter how reasonable it all sounded to me, it was impossible to ignore my rising emotions. I was scared.

By lunch time I was stressed out. I had a conference call with our west coast office at 12:30, so at noon I went downstairs to grab a sandwich and then ate in my office. Monika called while I was eating.

"How's it going?" she asked.

"Not so well. To be honest, I'm having second thoughts. But when I think about backing out, I feel like a coward."

"You're not a coward. And there's nothing wrong with changing your mind if that's what you think is right. But when we talked about it, you were pretty convinced that the right thing to do was to help CAGE. I think your emotions are influencing you more than you realize."

"I'm sure you're right. I still plan to go through with it, but I just wish it was over. Having all this time to think about it just fuels my fears. I've decided that this will be my last Generator treatment. I'm not sure if it's connected to my malignancy, but I'd rather not take any more chances." My computer was telling me that it was time for the conference call. "I've got to go Monika. I've got a conference call that's ready to start. I'll call you later. I love you."

"I love you, too. I'll be waiting for your call."

The call distracted me for the next two hours. By the time it was over I only had a few minutes to polish up some notes before leaving for the clinic. I was just about finished when the receptionist called me. "Dave, there is someone here to see you. His name is Harris and he said you know him. Should I send him up?"

I couldn't believe it. "Yes, send him up." I leaned back in my chair wondering what he was doing here. A couple of minutes later Kharis was knocking on my open door.

"Can I come in? Wow, nice office. You must be a high powered exec," he said glancing around.

"Just a tier or two below CEO," I said laughing. "Have a seat. What in the world are you doing here?"

"I thought you might like some company at the clinic today. Mind if I join you?"

I was amazed. "Are you serious? Don't you have better things to do?"

"I was thinking about getting a haircut. So if you'd rather be alone, I'll get going."

"You could use a haircut, but I'd appreciate your company. I have to say I'm feeling a little stressed about this."

"I thought you might be. I'll wait for you downstairs. When will you be leaving?"

"Give me about 15 minutes. There's a cafeteria on the 2nd floor if you want to grab some coffee or something to eat."

"Thanks. I'll see you in a few minutes."

I quickly finished up and then headed downstairs. Kharis and I walked to my car making small talk. As we started driving he asked, "You've been having second thoughts I assume."

"Now why would you assume that? I told you I would go through with it," I said, but I was taken aback by his comment.

"You said you were stressed and I imagine you're experiencing a little fear. And that's most likely due to thinking a lot about what might go wrong and the potential dangers. If I were you, I'd be questioning my decision at this point. But then again maybe I'm wrong. And in case you're wondering, I've taken a few psychology courses."

"You should consider becoming a psychologist; I hear it's a decent job. Yes, you're right I've been thinking about it all morning. You and your friend Proxy have done a good job of convincing me that the Generator isn't necessarily the benign implement of health and well-being that it's cracked out to be. I'm almost a convert."

When I said that, I had a strong urge to share with Kharis my story of conversion. I hadn't shared it with anyone yet, and I wondered if Monika should be the first to hear, but it felt like this was the right time.

"Kharis, on Monday I was reading the Bible. I read the verse in Ephesians where it says God has good works prepared for us to do and it seemed like he was speaking directly to me. I read it and reread it. Then it's hard to explain what happened, but I knew that God is real and that the Bible is true. Jesus is who he says he is, and I want to try my best to live the way he wants me to."

"That's all it took? You believed that quickly? I know it happens, but I thought it would take a while for you to believe. You seem pretty analytical to me."

"If you're trying to get me to reconsider, forget it. I know what I know," I said with a smile.

"No, no. I'm just amazed at how God got through to you so fast. I didn't expect it. I need to learn to put my prejudices aside and have a bit more faith. So how did Monika react?"

"I haven't told her yet. I was excited to tell her, but then I thought that there was a right time and place. I didn't want to make a mistake."

"You've got more wisdom than I did when I became a believer. I just blurted stuff out left and right and turned off a lot of my friends—and my parents. It took time to undo my well-meaning, but foolish mistakes. From what I can tell, I think you can talk to her and not worry about making a mistake. Tell her just what you told me."

"I guess you're right. Maybe I was just afraid of how she might react, I don't know. I'll try and talk to her soon. So why did you want to see me today? Is there something you need to tell me?"

"You were on my mind. I prayed for you this morning and thought about what you might be going through—I mean what it would be like if I was in your place. I thought it would be good to come see you and offer to go with you to your appointment."

"You barely know me. Is this what 'love one another as I have loved you' is all about?"

The traffic was bad and we didn't say anything for a few minutes as I concentrated on driving. We arrived at the clinic and after parking and turning off the car, I took a deep breath.

"Still worried?" Kharis asked as he took his Bible out of his backpack.

"I just want to be done with this. I keep wondering if the Generator is going to make the malignancy worse. It's scary."

Kharis flipped through some pages in his Bible and asked, "How are we doing on time?"

"I'm five minutes early. If you've got something you want to read to me, go ahead."

"Here, it's better if you read it yourself," he said handing me the Bible. He pointed and said, "This is the book of Philippians. Read verses six and seven of chapter four."

I read out loud, "Don't worry about anything; instead, pray about everything. Tell God what you need, and thank him for all he has done. Then you will experience God's peace, which exceeds anything we can understand. His peace will guard your hearts and minds as you live in Christ Jesus."

Kharis said, "God doesn't want us to worry. He really wants us to trust him to the degree that we can have his peace and not be afraid. But there's a battle that takes place in our minds. When we think about all the stuff that can go wrong, all the bad things that could happen, our feelings follow our thoughts. We feel afraid. But if we choose not to think on those things and instead pray and trust God, we can experience his peace. It works, but I'm not going to say it's easy. It's a lesson we have to learn over and over again. Try and bring God into your life, into your thoughts, as often as you can. The more you practice it, the better you'll get at it, and the more you'll experience his peace and joy."

"I should have known better. I've been letting my thoughts go wherever they wanted and didn't even think about asking God to help me with my fears. I thought I should be able to conquer them. Thanks, Kharis. I'm going remember that verse and make an effort to practice it when I start to worry." I looked at my watch and said, "Okay, it's time to check in. Let's go."

After checking in, they were ready for me almost immediately. I had my MiNDi in my hand so I wouldn't forget to send the message to Proxy. When the technician came to get me, I pushed the "Send" button. I went into the room to change into the hospital gown. While I changed, I was talking to God and noticed I didn't feel afraid anymore. When I was ready the technician had me scan-in, and then I lay down on the table. As he positioned the Generator arm over my abdomen, I closed my eyes and relaxed. Being under stress for so many hours must have tired me out, and I almost felt like I could fall asleep.

The technician said, "We're all set. Once last check of the program and we'll get started."

My thoughts were elsewhere. I was thinking of Monika, Lori, and Jasmine. I thought about how much I enjoyed life. I wasn't afraid of dying anymore, but I wanted to live. I must have dozed off for a few minutes because the next thing I remember the technician was saying, "That's it. You can go and change now."

I felt elated. I just needed to hand the devices over to Kharis and I was on my way out of the cave. Or so I thought.

When it was over and we were in the car, I gave the devices to Kharis and said, "That's it for me. It's up to you and CAGE now." Then I asked him if he wanted to join us for supper.

"Thanks! I'd really like to, but I want to get these devices to Taylor so she can start the analysis. Are you going to make it to the meeting with Proxy tonight?"

"I'll be there. Would you be able to come over for a meal on Sunday? I'll check with Monica to see if that works and let you know tonight."

"That would be great. My girlfriend is hard at work on her thesis and won't mind if we don't get together this Sunday. See you in a few hours."

As I drove home I decided it was time to talk to Monica about my decision to become a Christian. I got home earlier than usual so I prepared supper and had it ready by the time she walked in.

"Are those steaks I see? And wine? Are we going to celebrate again?" she asked.

"This time we can celebrate my last Generator treatment," I said.

"Did it go okay?"

"It went fine. What a relief to be done with it."

"You still have a meeting tonight though, don't you?"

"Yes, at 8:00. But no more Generator treatments for me."

"At least for the next month. Or did you mean longer than that?"

"I meant longer, but we don't need to discuss that now. I want to talk to you about something more important."

"Oh. Okay, you've got my attention."

"You grab the rolls from the oven and I'll pour the wine," I said.

We sat down and started to eat, then I began, "Last Sunday, I was hanging on every word Kharis shared. It all seemed to make sense—not just what he said, but some of the things I'd read in the Bible became clear. God wants us to believe in him and he expects us to put him in charge of our lives. I just couldn't quite figure out that believing part. You said it yourself: how do we get to the point where we don't have doubts. I wanted to make a sincere effort to seek the truth, so I had decided to read through the whole New Testament and to ask God to help me believe in him if he was real."

I continued, "Monday night after you went to bed I was reading the verses in Ephesians that Kharis shared with us. I happened to read a bit further and it was like God was speaking right to me, telling me he had a plan for my life. Maybe that sounds strange, and I wish I could explain it better, but all of a sudden I knew that God was real. I had this wonderful feeling of peace that I'd never experienced before. By the time I went to bed, you were already asleep. I've been meaning to talk to you about it, but I wanted to wait for the right time. So what do you think?"

"I can't believe it! It doesn't sound like you at all. You always research and analyze everything before making a decision. Don't you still have lots of unanswered questions?"

"A lot. But when I first met Kharis, he told me that he had found the answers to the important questions. Maybe I only have one answer, but that's enough. I'm sure that Jesus loves me and has accepted me. All the other questions are secondary. I wonder if I would have ever believed if I had to try and reason my way to God. It might work for others, but I'm not sure it would have worked for me. I'd always have one more question that needed to be answered."

"You sound convinced. I'd like to know how to get to that place. I've been asking God to help me."

"Like Kharis said, everyone has their own story, their own way of coming to faith. When it happens to you, it will be different than it was for me."

"I'm sure that's true. I'm really happy, and a bit envious, that it happened to you. I'm excited to see what God is going to do in your life."

"He's already done one thing that you won't believe."

"What's that?"

"I decided that I want to live the rest of my life with you. Will you marry me, Monika?"

She dropped her fork on her plate and her face lit up. "What? This is too much. I'm not sure I can handle all of this in one day. Are you sure about that? Because if you are, then my answer is 'yes.' I love you and want to stay by your side no matter what the future holds."

"I'm sure. Let's set a date."

Monika thought for a moment and then said, "What about next Sunday. Jasmine will be here and we can have a small wedding in our home. I'll call Lori and see if she and Caleb are free. I'll invite Emily and you can invite Owen."

"I thought you'd want something a little more elaborate. Don't you want to think about it?"

"You know I like things simple. I just want my family present at the ceremony. Afterward we can go to a restaurant for lunch and then come back to the house for cake and coffee. If you want to invite a few more people over for cake that would be fine."

"If that's what you want, then it sounds good to me. You know I don't enjoy big gatherings. We can discuss the details later; I have to leave for my meeting soon."

"Okay. You do what you have to do to get ready. I want to call the girls and tell them I'm getting married. Do you want me to . . . no, you should do that. But what if they ask why you proposed to me? I think we should talk to them together so you can explain how you became a Christian. You don't have to leave right now, do you?"

"I've got a half-hour or so. Let's call them."

Lori wasn't sure what to make of my decision to become a Christian. But when I told her Monika and I were getting married, she got excited and started talking a mile a minute. She wanted to decorate the house, and help Monika pick out a wedding dress, and do whatever else she could to make it the most memorable day of our lives. Monika got even more excited and the two of them talked for 15 minutes before I held up my watch in front of Monika.

"Lori, your dad has a meeting tonight and we need to call Jasmine. I'll set aside Saturday to go shopping with you. How about I call you back in an hour and we can talk some more."

"I'll be here. If you can think of anything else you want me to do, just let me know. Bye, Mom. Bye, Dad."

"I'll be sure and start a list. Bye, Lori."

We called Jasmine and she was thrilled that we were getting married, but she was a lot more curious about why I became a Christian. I shared briefly about meeting Kharis and how he gave me a Bible, and that I came to believe through reading it. I told her I didn't have time to share my whole story.

"You'll be here on Friday. I'll tell you the rest of the story then."

"Okay, I'll be patient. But I want to hear everything. I've been studying religion and philosophy lately and I've found lots of truths that I can believe in, but I haven't examined Christianity much. I'd like to know what the Bible has to say about the meaning of life."

"I'll look forward to one of our lengthy arguments—I mean discussions," I said teasing her.

"Me, too. Will you or Monika be able to meet me at the airport?"

"One of us will be there for sure. We'll let you know. Goodbye, Jaz. I'm looking forward to seeing you soon."

"It will be a short visit, but I'm excited."

When I finished talking to Jasmine I quickly changed, kissed Monika goodbye, and left for the meeting. The sun was low in the sky as I hopped on my bike. As I neared the coffeehouse, I saw Kharis getting off of the bus on the corner. I waited for him outside and we walked in together. Proxy was already sitting at a table. We sat down and Proxy asked, "Did everything go alright?"

Kharis answered, "Everything went fine. Taylor is working on the analysis. She said it should be ready by tomorrow morning."

"Good. The results will be the same as last time. Someone's been messing with the Generator formulas," Proxy said.

Kharis quickly sat up straight then leaned forward over the table. "What did you find?" he asked.

Proxy responded, "The formula has been deliberately altered. Thanks to your help, Dave, I was able to make a copy of the formula as it was being loaded into the Generator. I compared it to the formula we extrapolated from the data Dave captured last week. The formulas are identical. I guarantee that the data from today's session will match last week's data," Proxy explained.

"But how can you be sure it wasn't just a hardware malfunction?" I asked.

"The odds of a hardware malfunction producing the exact same error twice are astronomical—especially for something as complex as a Generator formula. And we have proof that the exact same formula was used last week and yesterday. The only possible explanation is that the formula was altered before it was loaded into the Generator. My hunch is that Future Health is behind this."

Kharis said, "I agree that someone is altering the formulas. But why would Future Health do that? They already have the patent on the Generator and copyrights on most of the formulas. They more or less have a monopoly on the whole market. Why would they run altered formulas on their own Generator?"

Proxy replied, "For money. And they no longer have a monopoly. Their strangle hold on the market has been loosened in recent years. Both Russia and Germany are producing Generators. And several medical companies are researching new formulas. In some countries, the government itself is funding research. If someone comes up with a formula to cure the common cold they'll be a millionaire overnight. Find a cure for malignancy and you'll be a multi-millionaire and win a Nobel Prize."

I interrupted, "Okay, there's lots of money to be made, and it's a mad race to see who can come up with the next great Generator cure. I still don't understand why they would secretly run formulas on their own Generator," I said.

Proxy replied, "I believe they are experimenting with new formulas to try and revive malignant cells. That's what current research is focused on. They are already running Generator experiments on live animals in Europe, and they are not far away from starting clinical trials. That gives them a huge head start in the race to find a cure for malignancy. Do you have any idea how long it takes to get through the approval process to conduct live experimentation on people here in the States—even for Future Health?"

I protested, "I admit that there's some logic to your argument, but you have absolutely no evidence to show that Future Health is behind it—it's pure conjecture. Just think of the risk they would be taking. If they got caught it could destroy the corporation."

"Not a chance. I mean not a chance that it would destroy them. They've got the best lawyers money can buy. They wouldn't be shut down. Sure, they would pay huge fines, but they can afford it. And just think how much money they could make with a cure for malignancy! Yes, it's a big risk, but the payoff is much bigger. Besides, they would likely blame some lower level executive or someone in the R&D department for acting without proper authorization. And who knows, that might be exactly what's happening. But let's say it was a decision that came down from one of the highest levels of the corporation. Do you think any of those guys would never be indicted? They're smart enough to cover their tracks. A few heads might roll, but the company wouldn't suffer much."

I nodded my head in agreement. "That much I can believe. How many times have we seen that kind of thing happen? It's wishful thinking to believe that justice would be done. So let's say Future Health wanted to test a formula on me. How would they do it?"

Proxy answered, "That's the easy part, and in my mind the reason they are the top suspect. They have Net access to the Generator. That's how new, approved formulas get sent to the Generator in the first place. Next, they would need to identify a malignancy patient for their experiment. They already have some access to data from the NHD, but it's possible that they had to hack in deeper to get the personal information they needed, or maybe not—after all they are a medical research facility. Regardless, they used the NHD to locate a malignancy patient, in this case, you. So when you scan-in for your Generator treatment, they can identify you—or rather some computer identifies you instantly and then instead of allowing the Generator to load the right formula, it sends some experimental formula over the Net to the Generator."

"In that case we should be able to see them coming across the Net as soon as a session is initiated. It wouldn't be hard to spot them, especially if we knew when they were coming. But we don't have the tools to run a trace. We'd need Guardian Security to help us. Are you planning to contact them?" Kharis suggested.

"No. At least not yet. We might have to eventually, but I have something I want to try first. There are two ways to get into the Generator, hack in or use the access codes. Hacking in is a serious challenge—I know I've been trying. And you need to be concerned that Guardian Security doesn't spot you while you're trying. I'm not saying it's impossible to do, and we can't rule it out, but it would take a very knowledgeable hacker to accomplish it. That's one reason I'm guessing, and hoping, that the access codes are being used to connect to the Generator," Proxy said.

"Why are you hoping the access codes are being used?" I asked.

Proxy explained, "Because when they're used the Generator automatically makes an entry in its logs. The log entry shows when the connection was made, what was done, and most important, who connected to the Generator. It's standard security procedure. Does that make sense?"

"Do you think the perpetrator would leave a fingerprint like that? A log entry would be evidence that could convict them. I'm skeptical," I said.

"Unless they wiped off their fingerprints before they left," Kharis said.

"You figured it out, my young Padewan," Proxy said with a smile. "Explain it to Dave."

Kharis explained, "Imagine that someone at Future Health, let's say a Mr. Smith, uses the access codes and clandestinely sends an experimental formula directly to the Generator over the Net. The Generator uses that formula for a single session, and when the session is over the formula is erased as usual. But the log entry would show what formula was loaded into the Generator and who sent it. A clear fingerprint so to speak. To remedy that, Mr. Smith opens the Generator's log file and falsifies the log entry to indicate the prescribed formula was used and that it was the clinic that accessed the Generator. Essentially, he wipes off his own fingerprints and leaves the clinic's fingerprints behind. So if someone checked the log, it would look like everything was normal. What Proxy wants to do is connect to the clinic's computer system and watch while this is taking place. He'll able to make a copy of the log entry before it gets modified, and then he'll have a record of who it was that really accessed the Generator. We won't need Guardian Security to run a trace."

"So when is your next Generator session, Dave?" Proxy asked.

I looked at Proxy not quite believing what I heard. "That was my last one. Didn't I tell you I'm starting a stem cell clinical trial next week? One of the conditions is I'm not allowed to have any exposure to the Generator during the four week trial."

Kharis looked at Proxy and said, "I thought you knew. But even if you didn't, how could you ask Dave to go through another Generator treatment? You know as well as I do that it's probably the reason he has malignancy. He's already put his life at risk to help us."

Proxy pleaded, "Dave, we need you to do this. Think about what it means. We could catch Future Health red-handed. An investigation would be started immediately."

I was frustrated. Proxy clearly understood the risk I would be taking. He seemed to have no regard for my situation or for me. I respected him for all he was doing to try and save lives, yet he didn't seem to care that I might be sacrificing mine.

"I'm sorry. I want to help, but I'm not going to miss my chance to participate in the trial," I said.

He looked straight at me and said, "Kharis told me you've become a Christian. Aren't you supposed to put others before yourself?"

Kharis with obvious anger in his voice responded, "That's not fair, Proxy. If you're trying to manipulate Dave, it will backfire. And what makes you qualified to advise us on matters of our faith? I think you need to get your priorities right. If you want us to believe that you care about people, then you can demonstrate it by showing concern for Dave."

Proxy sighed and spoke in a gentler tone, "Dave, I apologize. There's no excuse for what I said, but I've been trying to get these guys for years. You have no idea how hard it was when my brother-in-law died and left Maria alone with her kids."

"Maria? Do you mean Maria Moreno?" I said.

"Didn't you know she is my sister?"

"Nobody told me."

"There's not much family resemblance, but she's only a half-sister. We weren't real close growing up, and when I got involved with CAGE she thought I was some kind of extremist. A couple of years later her husband was diagnosed with cancer and was treated with the Generator. The cancer was cured and the two of them became closer than ever. Then they discovered the malignancy. He died within four months. She's been helping us ever since."

"I really would like to help. Something needs to be done. And you're right—Christians are supposed to help others. But I have a family to consider as well. I'm afraid I don't know much about the Bible yet and how all of this is supposed to fit together."

"I know. And I'm the last person to try and tell someone else what the right thing to do is. My life is hardly a shining example of virtue and self-sacrifice. We'll find another way. Maybe we'll take the evidence we've got and see what we can accomplish. It sure would be nice to catch them in the act though."

Kharis spoke up, "Dave you've had a long day and there's nothing more we can do right now. Why don't you go home and get some rest. I'll get in touch with you in a day or two."

"You're right, I'm exhausted. I'm going to head home. Proxy, it might not sound like much, but I'm going to be praying about this. Kharis, does Sunday at 5:00 work for you?"

"I'll be there. Thanks, Dave."

"Thanks for all you've done, Dave. I hope to see you again soon," Proxy said.

Chapter 16
Day 75 – Friday, May 23rd

I didn't feel much like going into work. I hadn't slept well and couldn't stop thinking about the previous day's discussion. When I told Proxy I wouldn't be having any more Generator sessions, I responded without even considering it. I wasn't expecting to face that question so I wasn't prepared. And I think I reacted to the way he naturally assumed I would be willing to subject myself to another Generator session. In my mind I was already on my way out of the cave. Was I supposed to go in deeper? I couldn't help but think about that verse in Ephesians. God says he has a plan for me. But how could I know what it is?

The day went agonizingly slow. I was anxious to get home and have the weekend to relax and think through everything. At 4.15 Dr. Steele called.

"Hello, Dave. Do you have a couple of minutes to talk?"

"Sure. Do you have the scan results?"

"That's why I'm calling. I've been looking over the scans and there's clear indication that the malignancy spread faster than normal again. But some of the previously infected areas have reduced in size slightly. I don't understand why it is spreading so quickly—it's baffling. But I think that the reason we're seeing some reduction in size of infected areas is because of our immune boosting protocol. Your immune system is fighting the malignancy and it appears that some cells are repairing themselves. Unfortunately, it isn't nearly fast enough to keep up with the outbreak of new cells being infected with malignancy."

"Has my 'M' status changed?"

"I'm sorry to say that it changed by three days. You are now M-72."

My fears were realized, but it didn't affect me like I thought it would. I was calm and still believing that the stem cell therapy would work for me. However, I was even more convinced that the Generator was responsible for the spread of the malignancy.

"Dr. Steele, I'd like to discuss some things with you about my treatment. I've had contact with a health advocacy group that believes the Generator could be responsible for causing malignancy. At first I was pretty skeptical, but as I've looked into it, I think there could be something to their claims. I'm can't be certain, but to be safe I would like to stop Generator treatments. Now that I'll be starting the stem cell therapy, do you think it would be alright to skip my treatment next week?"

"You start the trial on Thursday, right?"

"That's right."

"Then I'll agree to let you skip next week's session although I'd still recommend having one on Wednesday, or even early on Thursday before your hospital appointment. I'd be interested in discussing what you've learned about the connection between the Generator and malignancy sometime. I believe the Generator is safe. If the stem cell therapy doesn't work, I'd strongly recommend continuing the Generator protocol to try and boost your immune system. But at least for the next month or so you won't have to concern yourself about any more sessions."

"Good. It will be a relief not to have to think about it."

"I see you have an appointment at the hospital tomorrow. They'll be taking blood and tissue samples and giving you a basic exam. I don't foresee any complications, but we'll have to wait and see. I'll contact you on Monday if there's anything to report."

"Thanks."

"Only one week to go until you enter the trial. Keep your spirits up, Dave."

"I'm trying," I said. I actually did feel a little bit better knowing that I was done with Generator treatments for the next few weeks.

I called Monika on the drive home and shared the news with her. She tried to encourage me to look ahead and not worry about the reclassification to M-72. I told her I wasn't too concerned, but the truth was I was feeling discouraged. When I got home I asked her if we could wait until tomorrow to discuss wedding plans and she completely understood.

We were just sitting down to relax after supper when Maria called.

"Good evening, Dave."

"Hello, Maria. How are you?"

"I'm fine. I know you wanted me to keep you informed about the class action lawsuit. Based on the information we received today, it looks like we have a strong case. Our Washington D.C. office is working on the paperwork and it should be ready next week. Before our lawyer contacts Future Health, he plans to call the Ministry of Health and see what they have to say. I'd like to discuss the case with you further. It shouldn't take more than 30 minutes. Would you be willing to stop by my office early next week?"

"I think I can manage that. Can I call you Monday morning to arrange a time?" I asked.

"That would be fine. I hope to see you soon. Goodbye."

"Thanks for your call. Goodbye."

Monika asked, "What was that all about?"

"It sounds like the data has been analyzed and it must have matched the previous week's data. She said they have a strong case and are ready to file the lawsuit. Apparently one of their lawyers is going to call the Ministry of Health first to see how they respond. That would be the quickest way to get an investigation launched. But I seriously doubt that will happen. If the Ministry of Health won't listen to CAGE, Proxy recommends going straight to the press. I think that's the most likely scenario, but that's up to CAGE's lawyers to figure out."

"What have we gotten ourselves into?" Monika asked.
"A deep, dark cave," I responded.

Chapter 17
Day 71 – Saturday, May 24th

Saturday morning I felt much better. I had a lot to look forward to, and I wasn't going to let myself get discouraged. After breakfast Lori called to say she was almost at the house. Monika and I walked out to the porch to wait for her.

Lori pulled up a couple of minutes later, leaned out the window, and said, "Good morning, Dad. Do you want to join us? I'll have you home by suppertime, I promise."

"Shopping! You know me better than that. But thanks for the offer. Can you stay for supper?"

"What are you making?" Lori asked.

"How about your favorite gourmet fare: grilled cheese and pickles."

"With sharp cheddar?"

"Yup."

"Yum. I'll try and eat a light lunch so I won't spoil my appetite. See you around dinner time."

I kissed Monika goodbye and said, "Be careful! Remember you'll be alone with Miss Glamourista. She'll take you to the most expensive shops in town to look for a dress, and she might try and sway you into an extravagant reception or something. Just keep saying to yourself: I like to keep things simple, I like to keep things simple."

"Maybe you should come. I could use the moral support," she joked and walked toward the car.

"You two enjoy yourselves. I'll see you around suppertime."

"Thanks. See you later," Monika said as she got into the car.

After they drove off I called my brother, Owen.

"Morning, Dave. How are you doing? What's the latest news?"

I gave him the update on my health status.

"Are you handling it okay?" he asked.

"To be honest, I think I am so far. I'll probably fall apart if the stem cell stuff doesn't work though. But I'm no longer afraid of dying."

"What! Are you sure this malignancy thing hasn't affected your brain?"

I laughed. "It doesn't work that way. You might not believe me, but I've been on a bit of a spiritual journey and I found God."

There was silence. After several seconds he said, "Okay, I won't joke with you about something like that. But which God did you find?"

"The Christian one."

"So you believe in Jesus."

"Yes."

"That's cool. A guy at work is a Christian and I've got nothing but respect for him. I'd be interested in hearing how you decided to join a church and how you knew which one to pick."

"I didn't join a church. Hmm—haven't even thought about that yet. I may have to check that out."

"So how did you become a Christian then?"

"Do you want to grab lunch somewhere? I'd rather explain it in person."

"Barbeque?"

"And steak fries!"

"I'm in. How about the Brick Oven at 12:30?"

"Does 1:00 work? I've got an appointment this morning."

"I'll see you at 1:00 then."

"Good. See you there."

My appointment took longer than I thought. There were a lot more patients at the hospital than were typically at the clinic, and I wasn't used to having to wait so long. It was nearly one o'clock when they finally finished up with me, so I called Owen to let him know I wouldn't get to the restaurant on time.

"Hi, Owen. Sorry, but I'm running late. The nurse must have jabbed me a dozen times trying to find my vein. I finally recommended rolling up my shirt sleeve and then it went much better."

"Very funny. You know how I am about needles. Are you trying to ruin my lunch? So should I order for you?"

"Good idea. I should be there by around 1:15. You know what I like, right?"

"The baby back rib platter with extra sauce."

"My mouth is watering already."

Owen and I had a great time at lunch. It had been two years since we had last seen each other. We vowed that if I survived, we would make an effort to get together regularly. I was serious about it; I hoped he was, too.

He listened thoughtfully when I told him how I came to faith and asked a couple of poignant questions.

"I appreciate your listening ear. You've always been willing to hear me out without giving me a lot of grief about my choices," I told him.

"I'm your brother, not your dad. But if you remember, when we were growing up I used to give you a pretty tough time. Then after I went away to college I realized we all need to choose our own way and respect another person's right to walk their own path. I'm not sure where your path is going to take you. You've had some kind of spiritual experience and it seems real enough. But I'm curious to see if it will have a lasting effect. I'll give you some space to see if you feel the same way in six months or a year."

"Fair enough. Like Dad always said, 'words are cheap—let's see some action.' If I understand what the Bible says, then God is working in my life, inside of me, and living the Christian life is not something I have to do in my own strength. If I had to try and do this on my own, I'm sure I'd fall flat on my face. So I'm with you. I want to see where this leads as well."

"I'm glad to hear you say that. Dad taught us well."

"One thing has already changed—or is about to change. I asked Monika to marry me."

"Are you serious? Now why did you do that? Did someone tell you that if you're a Christian you need to marry her?"

"No, nothing like that. Monika brought it up so I checked it out in the Bible. I have to admit I don't completely understand it all, but it's clear that marriage is what God wants and that it's supposed to be a lifetime commitment. I'm sure that I love Monika and that the right thing to do is to marry her."

"Can't you love someone without getting married? I have several times."

"I suppose so. I'm just convinced that marriage is part of God's plan for us. Maybe I'll fail, or maybe Monika will want out at some point. But we'll cross that bridge . . ."

". . . when we come to it. Another one of Dad's favorite sayings. So this was really your decision and nobody pressured you?"

"Nobody."

"Then what can I say? I don't see why it will make any difference, but you know I've got your back little brother. I hope it will work out."

"So would you be my best man? We're getting married this Sunday at our house."

"Do I have to wear a monkey suit?"

"Just a jacket and tie. Think you can handle it?"

"I'm pretty sure I have one of those. I'll be there. Can I bring Amelia?"

"Of course. Are you sure you want to risk it? She might start pestering you to get married."

"Won't happen. What woman would want to get stuck with me for the rest of her life?" he said with a smile.

"Good point," I said as I picked up the check.

"If you know what's good for you, you'll give that to me. I'll let you buy me lunch when you have a clean bill of health."

"Okay, I'll take you up on that," I said and handed it to him. "It's amazing how nice everyone treats me when they know I've got malignancy. Maybe we should all pretend everyone has malignancy; it might be a better world."

"I think you're on to something there."

Lori and Monika returned by suppertime. Lori had to get home to Caleb, so we didn't have much time to talk. Monika had bought an elegant but practical dress—something she would be able to wear on other occasions. Lori talked Monika into a catered meal at the house instead of going to a restaurant, which I thought made good sense. And she promised to keep the decorating to a minimum. I told her I'd believe it when I saw it. Monika had ordered a cake, so it seemed to me we were all set.

"I'll be over on Saturday morning to see Jaz and get things organized. You won't need to do a thing, Mom," Lori said.

"Thanks for everything, Lori. And you better let me pitch in. I'm not going to sit around and let you and Jaz have all the fun," Monika said.

"Okay. But remember, I'm still in charge."

"Yes, ma'am. Whatever you say. See you Saturday."

"Dad, call me on Thursday to let me know how the stem cell thing went. Everything is going to be alright. Don't worry."

I gave her a hug and said, "It's all in God's hands. I'm not worried."

"I want to talk to you some more about that soon. Love you. Bye."

"I love you, too. I'll talk to you on Thursday."

On her way to the car she stopped, turned around, and asked, "You've got someone to perform the ceremony, right?"

Monika and I looked at each other. "I guess we need one of those, don't we?" I said and scratched my head. I said to Lori, "I'll make a few calls. If we have to, we can always use one of those Net marriage sites."

"Pulease, Dad! Do I have to do everything?"

Monika said, "Don't listen to him, Lori. He's just having fun with you. We'll find someone; don't worry."

"I would hope so. Try to be a little romantic, okay, Dad?"

"We could put some plastic flowers around the monitor. It would look nice," I said with a straight face.

"Okay, I'm leaving. He's all yours Monika. I don't know how you've stayed with him this long."

"Bye, honey" I said.

"Bye. See you soon," Monika said. Then she turned to me and said, "She might have a point there. I hope I'm not making a big mistake by agreeing to marry you."

"You're a comedian, too," I said and we laughed together.

Chapter 18
Day 70 – Sunday, May 25th

It was raining Sunday morning and I was happy to spend some time relaxing and reading. I read a couple of chapters in the Bible and then used Monika's DigiPad to look up references to the word "church" in the Bible. There were a lot. It didn't take long to see that it was a big part of the Christian life, and that bothered me a little bit. I'd only been in church for funerals and weddings up to that point in my life, so I'm not sure why I was prejudiced against them. I needed to at least research it further and be willing to visit one or two. But there were so many different ones listed in our community. How could I figure out which ones to visit? And the thought of going someplace where I didn't know anybody wasn't very appealing. I found some verses in the Bible about churches meeting in people's houses. That struck me as a little less threatening. I wonder how I would find one of those, or if they even existed anymore. But the whole process seemed like more than I could handle right now. I took a deep breath and told myself this could all wait until the stem cell trial was over. Then I remembered to pray and ask God to help me figure it out. I felt better about it after that, and decided that I didn't need to worry about it. I was going to trust God to lead me like he said he would.

Kharis showed up promptly at 5:00 holding a bottle of wine in each hand. "I brought red and white just to be sure," he said.

"Thanks. Come in and have a seat. I think dinner will be ready in a half an hour," I said.

Monika corrected me, "More like 20 minutes. Hello, Kharis. Glad you could make it."

"Hello, Monika. Whatever it is you're cooking, it smells fantastic. How are you doing, Dave? What's the latest?" Kharis asked.

I gave him the update on my new "M" status and on my decision not to have any more Generator treatments.

"Are you discouraged?" he asked.

"I was at first. But with the stem cell trial starting this week, I have to say I'm feeling hopeful. And when I do start to feel down, I try to remember to pray."

"That's good to hear. So you've decided to stay away from the Generator for good?" Kharis asked.

"It will depend on what happens after the investigation—assuming there is one. I need more assurance that it is safe."

"If we could only get the Ministry of Health to launch an investigation. Even with the evidence we have, our prospects are bleak. Maria and I have talked to three more people with malignancy in the last two days to see if they would be willing to help us, but they turned us down. We aren't giving up though."

"Do you think I should consider having another treatment?"

"I thought it wasn't allowed during the clinical trial?"

"It isn't, but I don't start until Thursday. I could have a session on Wednesday. My doctor even recommended one."

"If we only knew what the risk was. The formula they are using on you might be harmless or it might be the reason your malignancy spread so quickly. But I can't give you an objective opinion. You have your family to consider. Now if it was up to me . . ."

Kharis paused then I looked at him and said, "You were saying."

"Nothing. It's not my place to try and influence you to do something you might regret later. Besides, my opinion would hardly be unbiased. I've been with CAGE for over two years and when we're this close to our goal, there's nothing I'd rather do then catch these guys. The only thing I'll say is think about it, talk it over with Monika, and ask God for direction. If he wants you to do this, he can lead you."

"I suppose so, but I'd like to know how he'll let me know what to do."

"Just give him a chance and be willing to obey. That's all you have to do. My pastor likes to quote another pastor who had a simple formula for success: 'I pray and I obey.' One practical step you could take is to go ahead and schedule an appointment. That way you'll have the option of going through with it. I can make sure Proxy is ready to proceed on his end. Worst case: you call and cancel at the last minute. Would that work?"

"That makes good sense. I'll call my doctor tomorrow morning. That gives me three days to decide. So you attend a church?"

"Yes. I don't make it every Sunday, but I'm usually there."

Monika piped in from the kitchen, "Do I hear you talking about church in there? I want to get in on that discussion. Supper is just about ready, so let's sit at the table and talk while we eat."

We bombarded Kharis with questions during dinner. Most of mine had to do with church, while Monika wanted to know more about how to overcome her doubts. Kharis was flipping back and forth to read various verses in his Bible and I was writing them down so we could look them up later. He took some time to describe his church and some of the ups and downs of belonging to one.

"It isn't just a matter of finding a church where you get along with everyone and feel comfortable. That's almost impossible. You need to be convinced that belonging to a church is part of God's plan for you—and for all believers. Then you need to pick one and make a commitment to stick with it," Kharis explained.

"It sounds a lot like marriage to me," I said.

Kharis said, "There may be some similarities, but I like to compare it to being part of a big, extended family. And in a way, as brothers and sisters in Christ we are all related to each other. The spiritual bond we share binds us together."

The thought of finding and visiting a church felt a little overwhelming. "I don't know where to start," I said.

"I know it can be difficult to visit a place where you don't know anybody.

My church isn't very close to you, but you could at least come with me and visit, and we can take it from there," Kharis said.

That thought had crossed my mind, but I wasn't sure if visiting a church that far away was a good idea. I was relieved when Kharis suggested it. "Sure. That sounds good. But I'd like to wait a couple of weeks until things settle down some."

"No problem. Anytime you're ready, just let me know," Kharis said reassuring me. He looked at his watch and then said, "It's later than I thought. I have a bus to catch and need to get going." He put away his Bible and got up. "Thanks for a fantastic dinner and great conversation."

"You're easy to impress," Monika said. "Thanks for taking time to answer our questions. Unfortunately, I have more now than when you came."

"That means you're using your mind the way God intended you to. Without asking questions, we'll never discover the answers. I hope we can do this again. Maybe my place next time. I'm not very handy in the kitchen, but there's a great pizza place nearby," Kharis offered.

"Thanks, that's a tempting offer. Maybe we'll take you up on it," I said.

"Great. We can talk soon and figure out a day that works for all of us. I better hurry; I don't want to miss my bus. Goodnight."

"Goodnight, Kharis. See you soon."

Chapter 19
Day 69 – Monday, May 26th

After I got to work Monday morning I put in a call to Dr. Steele. I told him I was considering one more Generator treatment, and asked him if it would be alright to schedule an appointment even if I wasn't sure I wanted to keep it.

"No problem, Dave. I can tell you what's available. There are openings Wednesday in the morning at 9:30 or in the afternoon at 4:45, or on Thursday morning at 8:00. Which do you prefer? I'll schedule it for you right now," Dr. Steele said.

"Thursday morning at 8:00 would be the best. I've already got the morning off of work."

"Okay, hold on one second." There was a short pause then he said, "It's taken care of. Now I'm curious, what made you change your mind?"

"To be honest, I'm not sure what the right thing to do is. I just want to keep my options open. Will it be alright if I decide to cancel at the last minute?"

"They prefer a 24 hour notice, but under your circumstances I'm sure they'll understand if you can't manage that. It would be best to call the clinic to cancel in that case."

"I understand. Thanks, Dr. Steele. When do I need to see you again?"

"I've looked over the results of your tests at the hospital and everything looks good. Let's see how the first transplant goes and then I'll be in touch."

After finishing the call I pulled out my MiNDi and set an alarm for 6:30 on Thursday morning. That was my deadline for deciding to keep the appointment or cancel it.

Julia came by my office a few minutes before noon. We had rescheduled our lunch for today. "Are you ready to go?" she asked.

"I'm ready. You've got an umbrella. Does it look like rain again?"

"It's clouding up and they say it will rain this afternoon sometime."

I grabbed my umbrella and we headed out. Once we got outside I gave Julia a brief update on my status. She seemed disturbed. I told her, "I know it's more bad news, but I'm not too concerned yet. I start the stem cell trial in a few days and I'm anticipating good results."

"You're a strong person, Dave. Are you feeling okay physically?"

"A little less energetic than usual, but maybe that's just old age catching up with me."

"I've slowed down some myself these last few years. But is that one of the symptoms of malignancy?"

"My doctor said it can be. He said my immune system is working overtime to try and repair the cell damage, which might cause me to experience some fatigue. But really, it's hardly worth mentioning so far. I feel good."

"So, do you think the Generator is helping you?"

I wondered if I should tell Julia what I really thought and what had been going on. I felt like she deserved to know.

"I think there's a problem with the Generator," I said.

She looked at me with a shocked expression. "How did you come to that conclusion? Does it have anything to do with that law firm I told you about?"

"It's a long story. Do you mind waiting until we get to the café before I go into it?"

A few minutes later we were seated and had ordered our lunch. Then I explained what had been going on the last couple of weeks skipping over a lot of the details, but sharing how I had helped CAGE collect the Generator data.

"I'm not ready to say that it's the cause of my malignancy, but clearly something is wrong with the Generator and it needs to be investigated."

"It's hard to believe. I can't help but wonder if those problems were responsible for my sister-in-law's death."

"I know. But even if there is an investigation, we may never know the answers to those kinds of questions."

Julia was quiet for a few moments and then said, "When this news gets out to the media, it could open some of my brother's old wounds. I hate to think about what it might be like for him."

"I can understand how it could be difficult for him. But I'm sure you'll be there to help him through it if he needs you," I said trying to encourage her.

"I'll be there for him as much as I can be. Anyhow, it doesn't help to worry about it. He might have put all this behind him," Julia said.

"You're right. I'm trying to learn not to worry about things that are out of our control. But I've still got a long way to go."

"Me, too. So if you think there are problems with the Generator, are you going to stop your treatments?" Julia asked.

I wasn't sure if I wanted to explain that CAGE had asked me to have another session, and that I was still considering it. But I didn't want to lie to her either. I decided not to tell her about CAGE's role in my decision.

"I have a session scheduled this week, but I may end up canceling it. And once I start the stem cell trial, I'm not allowed to have any Generator exposure for four weeks."

"And you start the trial on Thursday, right?"

"That's right."

"You must be excited."

"I was trying to curb my enthusiasm, but gave that up. I feel like win or lose, this is my one shot at beating malignancy. All my eggs are in one basket, and if this doesn't work I'll be having a huge omelet for my last meal."

Julia looked at me, but didn't say anything. I didn't want her to.

"Hey, we're supposed to be celebrating, so let's have dessert! I'm buying lunch today and I don't want any argument."

"Okay, no argument. And dessert sounds marvelous."

I motioned for the waiter and asked him to bring over the dessert tray. Then I started talking about our upcoming wedding, and our moods became much more cheery.

After lunch I called Maria. "Hello, Ms. Moreno. I'm calling to arrange a time to stop by your office."

"Hello, Mr. Roberts. Thanks for calling. It would be good if you could stop by soon. Either this evening or tomorrow sometime."

I glanced at my calendar and said, "How about tomorrow. I could stop by at 12:30 or after work, around 6:00."

"The earlier time would be better."

"Alright. I've got it on my calendar."

"Thanks so much. See you tomorrow."

At supper I discussed with Monika my thoughts about having one more Generator session. She tried to keep an open mind, but she didn't think it was worth the risk. Even as we discussed it I felt uneasy. I was so relieved when I thought I was done with the treatments. If I agreed to another session, I knew it would be a stressful week as I anticipated it. Yet I couldn't help but feel like my job wasn't really over. Proxy had a good plan and with my help we might be able to catch the people behind this crime. But I didn't feel cutout to be a hero. My instincts for self-preservation were trumping my altruistic ideals. I was willing to help, but not ready to risk my life. And I saw the risk as being very real. So far stem cell therapy had not been tried on anyone who was classified as M-60 or lower. I was already M-69 and I barely made it into the trial. Another session might lower my 'M' rating and disqualify me, although I wasn't sure if they could kick me out now that I had been accepted. But that was another risk I might be taking. Maybe if God gave me clear guidance it would be different. I hoped I would obey him. But I didn't have that guidance, and I had doubts that he would give it to me, or more likely, that I would be able to recognize it if he did.

"I can understand why you don't want me to have another session, and to tell you the truth, I don't think I'm strong enough to choose to do it without clear guidance from God. There's still time for him to show me what to do, so let's wait before making the final decision," I said.

"I guess we can wait. It's hard for me to imagine what God could do to guide you though. It seems like we should use our minds to reason this through and make a decision," Monika said.

"Absolutely. I agree we need to think it through. But I want to leave room for God to intervene if he chooses to do so. This is all new to me and I'm not sure what that might look like either, but I want to be open to it."

"Alright. But if you think he is giving you some kind of divine guidance, will you discuss it with me before you make a decision?"

"Of course. And if we can't agree that God is directing me to have another session, I'll cancel my appointment."

"Okay. Then we just need to wait a little longer." She got up from the table and said, "Would you be willing to clean up after supper? I've got to call Lori to discuss some last minute wedding details."

"Sure. A mindless activity sounds pretty good right now."

"In that case, there's a pile of laundry that needs to be done, too."

"It doesn't sound that good!" I protested.

Chapter 20
Day 68 – Tuesday, May 27th

Tuesday morning I had my weekly meeting with my assistant managers. We finished around 10:30, and when I returned to my office I saw that Maria had called. I called her back right away.

"Good morning, Dave."

"Good morning, Maria. I see you called."

"I wanted to see if it would be possible for you to stop by this evening instead of at 12:30. There are some pressing matters that came up that require my attention."

"That would actually work better, since your office is on my way home. I can be there by 5:45."

"That's perfect. Thanks so much."

"You're welcome. See you soon."

After work I drove directly to the law firm. Maria came to greet me and brought me back to her office. She closed the door and before I could sit down she said, "Dave, CAGE was shut down by Guardian Security this morning. They showed up at our Washington D.C. office just as it was opening. They confiscated all our computers, told everyone to leave, and put locks on the doors. We don't have much information yet. We're making inquiries to see if it will be possible to reopen."

I was astonished. "What happened?"

"CAGE has been accused of illegally obtaining classified information from the National Health Database. I think they'll have a tough time proving that, but it has really set us back on our heels."

"Why did they decide to move against you now? It seems suspiciously coincidental."

"Not really. Our lawyers contacted the Ministry of Health yesterday morning and told them about our evidence that the Generator had malfunctioned. We've had some unpleasant encounters with them in the past and they weren't eager to talk to us. Our lawyers tried to force the issue, and hinted that the press would probably be very interested in examining our evidence. The person at the Ministry of Health said they would discuss it and get back to us in 48 hours."

"It looks like they got back to you much sooner than that."

"They're trying to scare us, or force us to waste lots of time and money in a court battle. We plan to have a conference call this evening to discuss our options, but for the time being CAGE is out of business."

"Are you planning to go to the press?"

"We'll discuss that tonight. If we decide to go that route, we would probably need your permission to identify you as the person who collected the data. Under the current circumstances, we're sure they'd be very careful to verify the source before presenting any information to the public."

"Is that why you wanted me to come to the office?"

"Not exactly. I planned to ask you to be the lead plaintiff in our class action lawsuit against Future Health. It's a huge responsibility and you wouldn't be able to remain anonymous. But it would give us a much better chance in court. Our firm was hoping to file the lawsuit in the next couple of weeks. Now we need to regroup and be a bit more patient—especially since I'm associated with CAGE."

"I'm willing to consider it. I'll need to find out what it involves and what my responsibilities would be. You realize I might not be alive in a couple of months."

"Yes, and forgive me for saying it, but if you should die, that would almost certainly give us a more sympathetic ear with the judge or jury. But that's not why we're asking you; I hope you understand that."

"Don't worry, I understand. I haven't met anyone else involved with the case, but I do trust you. When will you need an answer from me?"

"Given the present situation, it's hard to say. Anyhow, you have plenty of other things to think about this week. You start the clinical trial on Thursday, don't you?"

"That's right. And I'm getting married on Sunday."

"Oh my! I didn't know. Congratulations. Can I assume that you're marrying Monika?"

"Yes. After 23 years under a DLPA, we've finally decided we like each other enough to make a permanent commitment."

"With a track record like that, I'd be willing to bet that you can make it another 23 years—and I sincerely hope that you do."

"Thanks. My daughter will be in town until next Wednesday, so I'm afraid I'm not going to be available until after that."

"Sure. That's fine. I've put together some information that I can give you. Do you prefer paper or digital?"

"How about both."

"I'll have my assistant send the digital documents to you today. Here's the paper version."

I opened the envelope and pulled out a thick stack of papers. "Uh . . . do I need to read all of this?"

"No, not all of it. But you know lawyers; we need to cover all of our bases. I tried to summarize the main points in the first eight or ten pages. That will give you a good idea of what you might be in for. And just so you know, none of this will cost you anything. If there ever is a settlement, it could be substantial. But from what I can tell, I doubt monetary gain will be a factor in your decision."

"No, it won't be. I'll give it careful consideration." I stuffed the papers back into the envelope and said, "I'm sure you know that Proxy asked me to undergo another Generator session. I've been struggling with that decision, but I guess it's irrelevant now."

"No, I wouldn't say that. CAGE is temporarily shut down, but our volunteers will keep working in various capacities. And I imagine some of the staff will continue their efforts as long as they can afford to work without getting paid. Kharis only works part-time for us, and he's already said he wants to stay on the job as long as he can afford it."

"Proxy isn't on staff, is he?"

"No, he isn't. He started CAGE, but never took a staff position. Max, that's Proxy's real name, has never been paid anything, but he's still the driving force in our group. He told you we're siblings, didn't he?"

"Yes, he did. He explained about your husband's death. I was sorry to hear that."

"It's hard to believe it's been nearly three years. If anything good came out of his death, it was that Max and I started acting like a brother and sister should. He's been there to help me whenever I needed him. And that brings up another request: Max called this afternoon and said he and Kharis would like to meet with you tomorrow. He said it was urgent."

"I imagine he wants to ask me what my decision is about another Generator treatment. I have an appointment scheduled for Thursday morning, although I'm still debating whether I'll keep it or not." As I said that, a thought popped into my head. I wondered if I should ask Maria what her opinion was. Maybe God could use her as some sort of instrument in my decision process.

"I'm sure it's a difficult decision. Max has a forceful personality, but I'm sure you already know that. If he tries to pressure you, make sure you take a step back and collect your thoughts. You don't need to give him an answer on the spot. So will you be able to meet him?"

"I'm available. I don't look forward to another meeting, but I've come this far and I'm willing to hear what he has to say. Where and when does he want to meet?"

"He'll meet you at the coffeehouse. He said 7:00, but he said anytime after 6:00 would work if you want to suggest another time."

"No, 7:00 will be fine. Maria, can I ask you for your advice? What do you think you would do if you were in my shoes? Would you have another Generator treatment if you thought there was a good chance it would make your malignancy worse?"

Maria sat back in her chair and after a moment said, "If it were up to me, I'd help my brother. I still have a lot of anger about my husband dying of malignancy. If I had listened to Max when he tried to warn me, my husband might be alive today. If Max is right and Future Health is secretly using experimental formulas on patients, then they need to be stopped. I don't know if we'll ever catch the responsible parties, and I doubt that true justice will ever be done, but we need to try. What's more important is that we put a stop to their illegal and immoral acts and make sure something like this won't happen again. That's what I would do. But you also asked for my advice and your situation is completely different than mine. I'm sure you've thought it through and talked it over with Monika. Whatever you choose to do, I promise I'll respect your decision. You've already helped us and we're very grateful."

I listened carefully and agreed with Maria's plea for justice to be done. I sympathized with her loss and understood why she could still be angry. I was hoping to hear something that would be a clear answer to my prayer. But I didn't. I wasn't ready to change my mind.

"Thanks. I understand why you're angry, and I want to see justice done as well. I'll give it some more thought, but time's running out. I need to ask one more thing: do you know if my name was on any of the computers that were confiscated?"

"I doubt it. We've been very careful not to store any information like that on official computers. But it's highly likely that Guardian Security already knows that you and our law office have been in contact. They may even know you've been in touch with Kharis or Max. But you haven't broken any laws, and you don't have anything to hide."

"I hope you're right. But if they want to, I'm sure they could make life difficult for me. If Guardian Finance shows up at my door and says they want to audit my taxes for the last five years, it will be easy to connect the dots!"

Maria smiled and said, "That's unlikely, but you can be sure that we'll stand by you no matter what happens."

"Thanks. I'm not worried." I stood up to leave and said, "I want to know what's happening even if I have to stop by your office to find out. Is that okay?"

"Feel free to stop by, but call first to make sure I'm here. Otherwise I can have Kharis get in touch with you. If I need to get a message to you, I'll encrypt it. Thanks for coming in today. Take some time to consider our request."

"I will. I'll probably see you soon."

"Have a good night, Dave."

Chapter 21
Day 67 – Wednesday, May 28th

I woke up at quarter to six and knew that I wouldn't be able to get back to sleep. I got up and made myself some coffee, then sat down in the study with my Bible. My appointment at the clinic was just over 24 hours away and I hadn't made a final decision yet. If God was trying to show me what to do, I wasn't seeing it. I wanted to be done with it, to decide and not have to think about it anymore. But I needed to give it as much time as I could. I prayed and told God again that I was willing to do whatever he wanted, and asked him to help me know what that was. Then I read a few chapters in the Bible. I was reading in "Luke's Report" and most of it seemed similar to other things I had read. But there was a story that was new to me where Jesus was teaching about loving our neighbors. It astounded me. It was about a man who came across a stranger on the road who was robbed and beaten, and how he took care of his wounds, and then took him to an inn and paid for him to be looked after. I wondered what I would have done in that situation. I wasn't a particularly compassionate person and that bothered me. Was I ready to make sacrifices like this for others? Maybe I would for friends or people I loved, but what about strangers?

I thought about the opportunity I had right in front of me. I tried to compare myself to the man in the story, but mind was carrying on an internal debate. For one thing, that man wasn't risking his life, but I might be. And besides I had done something to try and help others. Didn't that show I cared? In the story the man left the injured man at the inn and then continued his journey. Maybe God was telling me that it was time for me to continue my journey and leave the rest up to CAGE. After a few minutes of thinking like this, I wasn't any closer to knowing what to do. Helping CAGE—and possibly saving many lives—was a noble thing to do. But I wasn't ready to risk my life for it unless I was certain that was what God wanted me to do.

It was nearly 7:00 and I needed to get to get ready for work. During the drive to the office I was feeling agitated and tried praying again. I wasn't afraid; I felt confused and unsure about how to approach this problem. After several minutes I came up with a plan of action: early tomorrow morning I would cancel my appointment at the clinic unless I had some clear reason not to. As much as I was able to, I put the entire matter in God's hands. After that I felt a little better, but deep down I still had doubts that God would be able to work this out in time.

It was an uneventful day at the office. It seemed that whenever my mind wasn't occupied with work, I would find myself re-evaluating my decision. I questioned whether or not I should even be asking God to direct me. Maybe he expected me to reason it out and come to my own conclusions. If that were true, then I knew I was in trouble! I barely knew what was in the Bible. How could I be expected to make a decision of this magnitude when I was so ill prepared? The mental gymnastics were exasperating. Finally in desperation I prayed, "God help! Help me know what to do! Don't trust me to do the right thing on my own. Don't let me mess this up." Then I did my best to stop thinking about it, and I was pretty successful at staying focused on my work the rest of the day.

It was a warm evening. I jumped on my bike and started to ride to the coffeehouse. "I haven't ridden this much in years. At least I'll be in pretty good shape if I die," I kidded myself. I rode at a quick pace and arrived ten minutes early. I had just gotten a cold drink and taken a seat outside when Kharis and Proxy came around the corner. They were talking to each other and they looked like they were happy about something. When they saw me they stopped talking. They joined me at the table and Proxy said, "Dave, I'm sorry."

I thought that was an odd thing to say. Then Kharis said, "It was all my idea. Please don't blame Proxy."

I was totally confused. "I have no idea what you're talking about. Who wants to explain?"

Proxy nudged Kharis and said, "He hasn't heard yet. You better do the talking."

Kharis nodded and said, "I'm sorry, we thought your doctor might have contacted you by now. He's going to wonder why the imaging scan was canceled. But you don't know what I'm talking about. Dave, Proxy and I have something to confess to you. We changed your appointment at the clinic to this morning and I took your place for the Generator treatment."

I couldn't believe it. I sat there stunned for several seconds before asking, "How could you possibly do that? And why would you?"

Kharis responded, "It was my idea. The last time you and I talked the idea just came to me. I discussed it with Proxy and we agreed that it wasn't fair to expect you to have another Generator session. The risk was too high and you have a lot to live for. It was important enough to me to risk undergoing one session so we could carry out Proxy's plan. And it worked."

I just sat there and stared at them. I was angry, and relieved, and confused. I wanted to hear what they discovered, but first I needed to hear about what they did.

"This is hard to take in," I said. "I want to hear what you found out, but start from the beginning and tell me the whole story."

Proxy spoke up, "Kharis, let me give him the abbreviated version. You can fill in the gaps if you want. Dave, Kharis convinced me that this was something he felt he had to do. He said he'd figure out a way to do it himself if I wouldn't help him, so I gave in and agreed to work with him. We faced a couple of risks. I already knew how to access the clinic's computer system, but it took me a while to figure out how to reschedule your appointment and also deactivate the messaging system, so you wouldn't be notified of the changed appointment. Did you notice that you didn't receive a 24 hour reminder of you appointment?"

"No. I didn't even think about it." The clinic always sent out a reminder a day before an appointment, but I hadn't received one and now I knew why.

He continued, "The other problem was getting our hands on a Bio-chip and getting it digitally signed. I know someone on the west coast who I contacted. She said she could manage it, but since we didn't have much time, I had to risk sending her your digital signature over the Net. Forgive me, but there was no other way. But don't worry, it was very securely encrypted."

"How could you possibly have my digital signature?" I asked in disbelief.

Proxy smiled and said, "Did you forget that I scanned your Bio-chip?"

I had forgotten.

"Once we had the chip with your digital signature installed, Kharis attached it to his right hand with some make-up putty. At the clinic he simply scanned-in and received your Generator treatment. Nobody suspected a thing."

When Proxy said that, what Kharis did struck me with greater force. It was possible that he could contract malignancy as a result of being exposed to the Generator—especially if he was treated by the same altered formula that was used on me.

I looked at Kharis. He must have believed that it was the right thing to do. Did God somehow direct him? I wanted to ask him, but not right this moment. I wasn't angry anymore, and I felt a deep respect and concern for him. "If this crazy scheme of yours results in you getting malignancy, I'll never forgive you—or myself," I said.

"Don't worry, I'll be okay. And even if I'm not, you have to forgive me—it's part of the deal," Kharis said with a wink. "Anyhow, we don't need to concern ourselves with that now. We have more important things to take care of."

"Your life is important. You're young and you have your whole life ahead of you," I said.

"Pray and obey—remember? The safest place in the world is in God's will," Kharis said.

I knew that was true, but I still questioned whether this was God's will for Kharis. It wasn't up to me to say if it was or wasn't; I was just having a hard time accepting the fact that God might allow him to contract malignancy. I wondered why God might do something like that.

"Okay, but I want to talk to you later about this. So, what did you find out?" I asked.

Proxy spoke, "Before we get to that, let me warn you to expect a call from your doctor. In addition to the treatment he prescribed, there was an imaging scan scheduled. I had to cancel that, otherwise when your doctor looked over the scan results it would be obvious that it wasn't your pancreas he was seeing. He won't know why the imaging scan wasn't run, but he might be suspicious."

"Thanks for the warning. I don't think he'll be suspicious. He's a bit absent-minded. He'll probably chalk it up to his own forgetfulness or some technical problem. So tell me what you discovered?"

"It was just as I suspected. After Kharis scanned-in, a formula was sent to the Generator over the Net—the same formula as last week. After the formula was sent, the log entry was modified. But I was able to make a copy of it before it was changed, so I have the Net address of the computer that sent the formula."

"So how do you track down the location of the computer?" I asked.

"That's not easy for me to do, so I contacted Justin, a colleague of mine who works for Guardian Security in D.C. I worked with him years ago. He knows all about CAGE and is sympathetic to our cause. He's going to get back to me in the morning with the computer registration information," Proxy said.

"I'm sure that's illegal, right?" I asked.

"Yes, it's illegal, but all he has to do is look up some information. He won't get caught," Proxy replied.

"Right. Hey, maybe we can all share a prison cell together," I said.

Proxy smiled and said, "You'll be okay; you haven't done anything wrong. You can come visit us."

"I'm an accomplice. So what's our next step?" I asked.

Proxy replied, "Wait until Justin calls. You start the clinical trial tomorrow morning so I was thinking Kharis could check in with you tomorrow afternoon. Where will you be?"

"I'm not sure. If I feel okay after the transplant, I might go to work. Otherwise I'll be at home in the afternoon."

"I'll call your office to see if your there. If not, I'll assume you're at home. If we've heard from Justin, I'll make sure to stop by and update you," Kharis said.

"Good. I'll be anxious to hear what you find out," I said.

"You've got a big day tomorrow. Go home and relax. Spend some time with Monika," Kharis said.

"I haven't had a chance to tell you that we're getting married this Sunday. You're both invited to the reception at our home at 2:00."

"Well, congratulations! I'll be there—if I'm not in jail," Kharis joked.

"I'll do my best to try and make it. If I don't get there, you can be sure it was for a good reason," Proxy said.

"Okay. I'll see you tomorrow, Kharis, and hopefully I'll see you soon, Proxy."

As soon as I got home I told Monika what happened. She was utterly amazed. "I can't believe it. Why would Kharis do that? What was he thinking?" she said.

"He said he believed it was God's will. It's pretty tough to argue with that response, isn't it? I wanted to question him about it, but it didn't seem like the right time."

"I want to hear what he has to say about that, too. Do you think there's a chance he could get infected with malignancy?"

"I'm sure there's a chance that he could—especially if he was treated with the same experimental formula that I was. But he's young and healthy. Maybe his body will be able to fend off any negative effects. Time will tell."

"Even if God was somehow directing Kharis to do it, it took a lot of courage. I hope nothing bad happens to him," Monika said.

"I'm not sure I could handle it if he got malignancy."

"Dave, you aren't responsible. It was totally his decision."

"I know, but what if I had agreed earlier to have the Generator session? Then Kharis wouldn't be in this predicament."

"You don't know that for sure. Kharis might still have done exactly the same thing. There's no point in blaming yourself."

"I suppose you're right. But as strange as it may sound, I seem to feel better about myself by feeling a little guilty."

"Even if you did something wrong, which you didn't, doesn't the Bible teach that we are supposed to forgive ourselves? What's to be gained by feeling guilty?"

"You're right again. Why do I bother to argue with you? I'd make a lousy lawyer."

"Yes, you would. Case dismissed!"

Chapter 22
Day 66 – Thursday, May 29th

It took me a long time to unwind and get to sleep after so much excitement, but I slept late the next morning and felt well rested. Monika took the day off and had breakfast waiting for me. When I walked into the kitchen I saw her on the couch reading.

"Good morning. How did you sleep?" she asked.

"Once I finally fell asleep I slept soundly. I feel okay."

"Are you excited?"

"I think I used up most of my emotional energy yesterday. But yes, I guess I'm a little excited. What are you reading?"

"I'm reading the Psalms. They're fantastic! You know how I love poetry. If you need an emotional boost, I would recommend reading them. I've marked down some of my favorites."

I had heard of the Psalms, but I wasn't particularly fond of poetry so I hadn't tried reading them yet. But Monika made them sound appealing, and I wondered if I had been missing something. "Thanks. Maybe I'll read some while I drink my coffee. We've got a good hour before we need to leave."

Talking about the Bible reminded me of Kharis. I had forgotten to tell her that I invited Kharis and Proxy to the reception. "I hope you don't mind me inviting Kharis and Proxy, that is, Max, to our reception. It seemed like the right thing to do, especially since we'll probably go to prison together."

"You're not usually this funny before breakfast. No, of course I don't mind. And I'd like to meet Max. He sounds like quite a character. What about Maria? Did you invite her?"

"No, I haven't, but I should. I'm not very good at this kind of thing. You should be in charge of the guest list. Any other suggestions?"

"No. We're trying to keep it intimate, remember?"

"Did you invite your boss?" I asked.

"I did, but she's out-of-town this weekend. I invited my co-worker, Dawn. You've met her a couple of times. We have lunch together almost every day. She always asks how you're doing and how I'm handling everything. I feel closer to her than to my sister sometimes. So I think we're looking at a dozen guests more or less—I mean for cake and coffee."

"That still qualifies as intimate in my book. Are you okay with it?"

"It's just right. Alright, I'm going to shower and get ready." She handed me her DigiPad and said, "If you're interested, try reading the Psalms that I bookmarked."

I finished eating and then took my coffee into the study to read for a few minutes. I opened the Book of Psalms and started to read from the beginning. They were short and it didn't take long to read several of them. Each one was unique, but there were some common themes running through most of the ones I read. The thing that immediately struck me was the type of language that the author used, and the degree of emotion that was expressed. He didn't hold anything back, but poured out his innermost thoughts and feelings directly to God. I wanted to have that type of relationship with God, too, but I had to admit that I was hesitant to express certain things, like anger or doubt, to him.

Another thing that struck me was how often the author cried out to God for help, or protection, or to be rescued. I could easily relate to those kinds of prayers. All my life I had been taught to be self-sufficient and independent. But what I really wanted was to have someone who would help me get through life. Someone who I could trust and who I knew would not let me down. I knew that it would take time to develop the kind of relationship with God that the writers of the Psalms had, but that's the direction I wanted to head.

We got to the hospital and were met by Ms. Hamilton, the head administrator of the clinical trial. She was very pleasant and put us at ease immediately. She told me that that process involved minimal pain and the chance of side-effects was negligible. I had already read that, but I didn't mind being reassured. She went over the schedule for the next four weeks and asked if I had any questions. I didn't, so after signing half-dozen forms she had someone lead me to an examining room. After changing into a hospital gown a nurse came in and checked my heart rate and blood pressure. She asked me if I wanted a tranquilizer and I told her I didn't. Then I lay down on a table and she applied a numbing agent to my abdomen above my pancreas.

She said, "Okay, in 20 minutes you'll be done. A doctor will be with you in a couple of minutes."

A few minutes later a doctor and nurse came in and prepared to give me the injection. The nurse positioned the ultra-sound machine and the doctor picked up the biggest syringe I had ever seen. Why hadn't I said 'yes' to that tranquilizer?! I closed my eyes and tried to relax. Then I tried praying. I was still tense. It hurt more than I thought it would, but it was over in just a couple of minutes.

"You look a little white Mr. Roberts. Are you feeling nauseous?" the doctor asked.

"A little, and a little light headed."

"Just take deep, regular breaths. It should pass in a minute or two. You did just fine. When you're ready, the nurse will lead you to a recovery room. You can sit or recline there. Don't walk around for the first 30 minutes. We'll check on you in an hour and if everything is alright, you'll be free to go."

Within a few minutes I was feeling okay other than my abdomen being pretty tender. Monika joined me in the recovery room and the time passed quickly. We were out of the hospital before noon. I thought I felt good enough to go to the office, although Monika tried to talk me into going home to rest. I turned my MiNDi on as we walked to the car and saw that I had a message to call Dr. Steele and also Maria. I decided to wait until I got to work to call them. I took Monika out for lunch, but I didn't feel like eating. Afterward she dropped me off at work.

"I'll be here at 5:00 sharp. Promise me you'll call if you feel like coming home sooner," she said.

"You can count on it. But I feel pretty good. Thanks for coming today. It was almost like a date."

"Half a date. You didn't eat a thing. Will you call and let me know what you feel like eating for supper?"

"I'll call, but right now the thought of food is a bit revolting. Maybe just some fruit."

"Fruit salad?"

"That would be great. See you soon."

On my way to my office I stopped by Julia's office. She wasn't in, but I left a message with her assistant. I got to my office and closed the door, then placed a call to Dr. Steele. He wasn't available, but I was told he would call me back shortly. He called within 20 minutes.

"Good afternoon, Dave. I see you're at work already, so the transplant must not have taken very long."

"I was in and out in less than two hours. They told me subsequent appointments will only need to be an hour. It's hard to believe it could be so quick and easy."

"And effective. It's a modern miracle. Are you feeling okay?"

"I'm fine now. Just a sore spot on my abdomen. That was a quite a harpoon they poked me with. My brother would have fainted for sure."

"To be honest, I don't like being on the receiving end of a hypo either. The other reason I'm calling is that there was some sort of problem at the clinic yesterday. Your imaging scan was not performed and when I followed up on it, I was told there was a cyber attack on the clinic's computer system yesterday morning. That might be the reason for the error. But it wasn't essential to have it done at this time, so there's no need to be concerned. Since you've started the clinical trial, we won't be able to reschedule it. You'll have an MRI next week, so we'll just have to wait until then to see how you're doing."

When he said there was a cyber attack on the clinic's computer system, I tensed up inside.

"Do you have any idea why would someone want to break into a clinic's computer system?" I asked.

"They're trying to figure that out. It appears they didn't steal any patient information, so you don't have to worry about that. They'll let me know what they find, and if it's anything that concerns you, I'll certainly let you know."

"Okay, thanks. Anything else you wanted to talk about?"

"Your next transplant is scheduled for next Thursday at 10:00. We need to schedule an MRI within a couple of days after that. The MRI appointment will be for an hour. Do you want to schedule it now?"

"Is the MRI at the clinic or the hospital?"

"We don't have an MRI machine at the clinic anymore so it will have to be at the hospital."

"Okay, then how about Thursday right after my transplant? I'll already be at the hospital. I've got the morning off, but I can take part of the afternoon off if necessary. By then it won't matter much how much time I take off since I have to inform HR of my M-60 status on Wednesday."

"Oh, that's right. We were so close to possibly avoiding that. Have you contacted any lawyers about joining a lawsuit yet?"

"What do you mean?"

"Haven't you heard that there is a legal battle brewing over the 'M' status notification requirements? I've read that a discrimination lawsuit has already been filed. You should look into it."

"Thanks, I'll do that." Great. Another lawsuit. I wondered if I could start a new career as a plaintiff.

"Alright, you're all set. I have you scheduled for 11:30 next Thursday morning. I'd also like to see you soon after that. Can I transfer you to Anne so you can schedule an appointment?"

"Sure."

"Okay, hold on a second."

When I finished speaking with Dr. Steele's receptionist I returned Maria's call.

"Dave, I'm glad you called. I have some new information to discuss with you and was wondering if you could come to my office this afternoon."

Proxy must have heard from Justin. I was anxious to hear what they found out, but didn't feel up to taking public transportation to her office.

"What about 5:30 or quarter to six? I'm without a car today and after just having my first stem cell treatment, I'd prefer not to do a lot of walking."

"Oh, I'm sorry; I didn't know. Did everything go okay? How are you feeling?"

"It went well and I'm feeling fine, just a little sore."

"I'm glad to hear it went well, and I understand if you'd rather not come in at all."

"No, no, I want to come. If I had my car, I'd come this afternoon, but I'd rather not use public transport."

"I understand. If you are interested in coming this afternoon, I'd be happy to send someone to pick you up. Otherwise I'll look for you at 5:30."

She was being persistent and I was getting more and more curious to find out what had been uncovered. I quickly checked my schedule and saw that I didn't have anything pressing in the afternoon. Work could wait.

"If you're able to give me a lift, then I can come anytime. What time should I expect the car?"

"It will be out front in 20 minutes. Thanks so much, Dave."

I finished up a couple of things before leaving. On the way out I walked pass Julia's office and she was at her desk.

"Dave! I didn't expect you to be in. Didn't you start the stem cell trial today?"

"Yes, this morning. Nothing to it other than the large hole the syringe left in my abdomen. Sorry, you didn't need to hear that."

"It's okay. That kind of stuff doesn't bother me. Did it hurt much?"

"It wasn't bad at all. Julia, I wanted to talk to you about something, but I'm on my way out to meet someone. I should be back by late afternoon. Will you have time to talk?"

"I've got a meeting that will likely run until 5:00. Can it wait until tomorrow morning?"

"That will be fine. What time?"

"I should be in by 7:45 and I'll be in my office until around 10:00."

"Okay, I'll come by at 8:00 tomorrow morning. Thanks."

"When will you know if the stem cell therapy helped?"

"They said I could see results in a week, but not to be disappointed if it takes longer."

"That's not too long to wait."

"No, it isn't. I'm still amazed at how fast it's supposed to work. I've got to go; I'll see you in the morning."

"Okay, see you tomorrow."

By the time I stepped outside, the car was there waiting for me. Twenty minutes later I was walking into Maria's office and was pleased to see that Kharis was also there.

"Dave, thanks for coming," Maria said.

"Maria told me the stem cell transplant went well. You'll have to tell me all about it just in case I need it sometime," Kharis said with a grin.

I wasn't too amused. "That's not very funny. You better take good care of yourself. If you contract malignancy I'll be pretty upset with you."

"Sorry. Not the time or place for black humor. I'm glad to see you. It's hard to believe you just had a transplant a few hours ago. Pretty amazing stuff."

"It sure is. So tell me, did you hear from Justin?"

Kharis replied, "Proxy got a call from him this morning. He's got the location of the computer that was used to connect to the Generator."

"Was it Future Health?"

"We don't know. The police have Max in custody," Maria said.

"What! When did that happen?"

"This morning. He called at 11:30 and asked me to send a lawyer to the precinct where he's being held for questioning."

"What happened? Is he under arrest?"

"I heard a brief report and it looks like he's going to be charged for breaking into the clinic's computer system," Maria explained.

"How serious is it?" I asked.

"We probably won't know for a few days. He didn't steal anything or cause any damage, and it's his first offense, so if he cooperates he might get off with probation," Maria explained.

"I never thought he would get caught. He seemed to know what he was doing," I said.

"He knew what he was doing. He wanted to get caught," Kharis said.

"Do you mean it was intentional? How do you know that?" I asked.

Kharis responded, "I'm pretty sure it was, but I don't know exactly why. He was angry that CAGE's board of directors hadn't gone public yet with the evidence we collected. He considered going to the press himself, but after we talked it over we came to the conclusion that doing that might make the Ministry of Health even angrier. He didn't want someone else to have to pay the price for his impulsiveness. But I don't know how getting arrested will help anything."

"They'll probably hold him overnight, so we won't know anything more until tomorrow. I'll have our lawyer bring him to the office as soon as he's released. That should happen first thing in the morning. Will you be able to join us?" Maria asked.

"I think so. Call me when you know more." I said.

"I will. I'll have my driver take you back to work or home if you prefer."

"Thanks. I think I'm ready to head home."

As I was walking out of the office I remembered I was supposed to invite Maria to the wedding. I turned and said, "Maria, Monika and I would like to invite you to our wedding reception this Sunday at our home."

Her face lit up and she said, "I'd love to come! Thanks so much for the invitation. It will be nice to celebrate with you and get my mind off of everything that's happened these last few days."

"The reception is at 2:00, and feel free to bring a guest."

"Thanks again, Dave. I hope to see you tomorrow. Maybe we'll have some degree of resolution by then," Maria said.

"Wouldn't that be nice," I said as I turned to leave.

I called Monika to let her know I was on my way home. She was surprised and wanted to know if I was feeling okay. I told her I was fine, but feeling pretty hungry. "Will you make me some waffles for supper?" I asked.

"Waffles? Sure, but you know you're not allowed to have syrup," she said.

"I know. I plan to smother them in applesauce. I'm starving."

"I'll have them ready by the time you get here."

"Great. And in between bites I've got some interesting news to share with you," I said.

Chapter 23

Day 65 – Friday, May 30th

I arrived at work early and as I was walking to my office, I saw Julia coming down the hall. She saw me and walked over.

"Good morning, Dave. How are you feeling today?" she asked.

"I'm still a little sore, but other than that I feel good. Do you have time to talk now?"

"Yes, I've got time. Let's go to my office."

As we walked to her office she asked how the wedding plans were coming along. I told her that my daughter Lori was in charge so everything was running like clockwork.

"She runs a pretty tight ship," I said.

"Then she must take after you," Julia said.

"She surpasses me in that area."

"Well, if she ever needs a job, tell her to look me up," Julia said with a smile.

I waited until we stepped into my office and closed the door, then I said, "You might need to replace me soon. Just so you know, I'll be M-60 next Wednesday and I have to notify HR."

"Yes, I know. I've been keeping track. Is that what you wanted to talk to me about?"

"Partly. I've been working on a transition plan so my replacement will have an easier time stepping into my position. I want to run it by you when I'm done, but it's not quite ready yet. I've also scheduled a meeting for my department next Friday. That's when I plan to break the news about my M-60 status."

"Do you want me to be there?"

"I'd sure appreciate it. It's scheduled for 2:00, but I can change it to fit your schedule."

Julia turned to her monitor and then said, "I'm free at 2:00 but have a meeting at 3:00. Will one hour be enough time?"

"More than enough. Let's plan on 2:00 then. One last thing: I've learned that a discrimination lawsuit has been filed to challenge the law requiring 'M' status notification. I want to contact someone about it and get more information. Have you heard anything about it?"

"Just that there are a number of people unhappy with the law. I can understand why. I think you should look into it."

"I don't want to cause trouble for the company, but I think it's worth checking into. I'll let you know what I find out."

"If there's anything I can do to help you, let me know."

"Thanks for being so supportive. You always are."

"I'm against the law and think it should be challenged. So, is today the day Jasmine is coming?"

"She flies in at 4:20. I plan to meet her."

"You must be excited? How long since you've last seen her?"

"Last August. It will be great to have her here for the wedding. Will you be able to come?"

"I wouldn't miss it."

"Good. That's all I wanted to discuss with you." I got up and walked to the door then said, "I'll try and get a copy of my transition plan to you by Wednesday. Any candidates for my position yet?"

"I was trying to avoid that discussion. I'd like you to give me some recommendations from your department, but let's put it off for at least a week."

"I've got the list ready," I said.

"I should have known. But I still don't want to see it until next Friday, okay?"

"Then I'll give it to you at the meeting," I said.

I hadn't heard from Maria by 10:30 so I called her. She answered and said, "Sorry for not calling you, Dave. Max is no longer in custody. He is trying to work out some kind of deal with Guardian Security. He said he would try to come to the office this afternoon. Do you want to stop by to talk with him?"

"It depends on what time he gets there. I'm picking up my daughter at the airport, and I need to be there by 4:30. Did he say anything about a computer registration? Justin was supposed to let Max know about that."

"Yes, Kharis wanted to know as well. The computer that was used to send the formula to the Generator is registered with Future Health."

"So Max was right. Future Health has been secretly using experimental formulas on me—and who knows how many others."

"Max said we can't be sure about that yet. Apparently they need to take another step to verify the formula was actually sent from that computer. He's been discussing that with Guardian Security."

"Does that mean someone has to undergo another Generator session?" I asked.

"I don't know. He said he'd explain it to me this afternoon."

"Then I'll try to come. Can you call me when you know when he'll be there?"

"I'll contact you as soon as I find out."

"Okay. Then I'll see you this afternoon," I said.

Just before 3:00 Maria called to let me know Max and Kharis were on their way to her office. I decided to leave right away so I would have a few minutes to talk to them before leaving for the airport.

As I drove to Maria's office, I checked to see if Jasmine's plane was on time and found out it was running a few minutes late. That took some pressure off me, but I would still only have a few minutes to talk with Proxy. I was anxious to hear what happened to him, and find out what would happen next. Even if I was a few minutes late meeting Jasmine, it would be worth it to satisfy my curiosity.

I got to Maria's office and Proxy and Kharis were already there.

"I thought you'd never get here," Proxy said as I walked in. "Maria wanted to wait until you arrived before I explained what's happened."

"Okay, I'm here. Talk fast, because I have to leave for the airport in 20 minutes," I said giving Kharis, and then Proxy, a vigorous handshake. "Glad to see they let you go. That was a mistake. Are you planning to flee to Mexico?"

"Depends on whether or not they agree to my deal," Proxy said.

"And what would that be?" I asked.

"They help me catch the real bad guys," Proxy replied.

"I want to hear about that, but tell me something first: Kharis thinks you intended to get caught. Is that true?" I asked.

Max snorted and said, "I don't consider myself to be a professional hacker, but breaking into a health clinic's computer system isn't a serious challenge. It would have been easy to get in and out undetected, but I had to be sure that Guardian Security would be able to track me—and do it quickly. So yes, I made sure they would see me and could find me."

"But why?" Maria asked.

"Sorry, Maria, but it was time for me to take matters into my own hands. You know that it isn't very likely that CAGE's board will release the evidence to the press. It seemed to me like they're just trying to protect their own jobs. But Kharis convinced me that there is more to it than self-preservation. They have families to consider and probably other good reasons for not further antagonizing the Ministry of Health. So I came up with an idea to involve Guardian Security. I knew the easiest way to get their attention was to let them catch me. And it's working—so far."

"So far?" I asked.

"Unfortunately, I didn't have much to bargain with. I offered to confess to the crime, and I offered to show them some security holes in the clinic's computer system if they would listen to my story."

"And they agreed to that?"

"Not exactly. They said they already had enough evidence to convict me of the crime, and that it wouldn't take their cyber division long to figure out how I broke in. So they didn't have anything to gain. Fortunately, one of the agents was curious and wanted to know why I broke into the clinic's computer system. He said he would listen to my story, and if I had anything of value to say, he would make a note of it on my record. He told me it might help me when I was sentenced."

"So what did you tell him?" I asked.

"I told him what we had been up to, and that we had evidence to prove the Generator formulas were being tampered with."

"But couldn't you have told Guardian Security that without getting arrested?" Maria asked.

"Maybe. Maybe I could have gotten an appointment with some entry level clerk in a week or so. But here I was with two experienced agents listening to me—no appointment needed. I still didn't know if they would believe me, or more important, be willing to do anything with the information I shared with them. But I had their attention, and when I was done explaining, they left the room and told me to wait. About a half-hour later another guy came into the room. He was abrupt. He said that I had received a message from a public Net address located in Washington D.C. today and he wanted to know who it was from and what it said.

"That was the message from Justin," Kharis commented.

"Right. I figured they had been watching all my Net traffic. I had my bargaining chip, or at least I hoped so."

"What do you mean?" I asked.

"I've already told you Justin is sympathetic to our cause. He sent me the registration information for the Net address I sent to him. All our messages were encrypted, so Guardian Security wasn't able to read them. And Justin used a public computer to send the message so it couldn't be traced. He included part of a familiar quote at the end of his message. 'We humans do, when the cause is sufficient, spend our lives. We are when the cause is sufficient, insane'. He was letting me know that he believed in our cause and that he was willing to help. But I had to talk to him to see what degree of commitment he was willing to make."

"So you called him?"

"Not from their office. I told the agent that the message was sent from someone who works for Guardian Security who had helped me. Then I told him that I would decrypt the message for him, but first I needed to talk to that person privately. He left the room and then Trudy, the lawyer you sent came in. We spoke privately and I told her what I was up to. She advised me not to say anything more, and that we needed to take some time to figure out our options. Then two people came to talk to us and there was a lot of negotiating. At that point things got a little complicated and Dave doesn't have time to hear the details. In short, Guardian Security agreed to hold off on formal charges until next week. They are very interested in knowing if someone is tampering with the Generator formulas, and they want to see what kind of evidence I have. The only thing we haven't come to terms on yet is what to do about Justin. They want to know who fed me the information, and I refuse to give them his identity."

"Did you talk to Justin?" Kharis asked.

"Yes. I just spoke to him before coming here."

"So did you get any more details about the computer registration?" I asked.

Max replied, "No. All he could tell me is that it's a corporate registration and I'm sure Future Health has hundreds of computers at their Atlanta facilities where this one is registered."

"Does that mean we can't find out which one was used or who used it?" I asked.

"That's where Guardian Security comes in. I don't know how they'll react when I inform them that the computer used to send the unauthorized formulas is registered to Future Health. I'm heading over to talk to them when I finish up here. I'm hoping they'll be willing to conduct a sting operation like we did," Max said.

"And what if they aren't willing to do that? Or what if they can't get permission for the operation?" Kharis asked.

"I have some other ideas. But once I show them the data we captured and the log entry, I think they'll be convinced and willing to act. They know that if they can arrest the people behind this, it would give a huge boost to Guardian Security's public image. And they can use all the help they can get in that department. Besides, I already warned them that if they don't do something soon, the information would likely be passed on to the press, and that would result in another embarrassment to their agency," Proxy said.

"I'm anxious to see their response. You're a tough negotiator," I said. "I'm afraid I need to leave to meet my daughter. Will somebody get in touch with me and let me know what happens after Proxy meets with Guardian Security?"

Kharis responded, "If we know anything by tomorrow, I'll come by your house. Otherwise I'll see you on Sunday."

"Thanks. Do we still need to be careful about electronic communication?" I asked.

Maria responded, "Yes, we do. You can be sure that anyone associated with CAGE is under observation right now. Anything sensitive needs to be discussed face-to-face. I know it's inconvenient, but it's better to play it safe."

"Alright. I've got to run. See you soon," I said and got up to leave.

Jasmine called me just as I got to the airport. A few minutes later I saw her smiling face coming toward my car. I jumped out and she waved excitedly and shouted, "Dad!"

As I gave her a hug and took her luggage she said, "It's so good to see you. It's been too long since I was home. You look great? How are you feeling?"

"Pretty happy right now. I've been looking forward to your visit for weeks. You look wonderful. Fit and tan. A little on the skinny side, I'd say."

"It's all muscle! I get lots of exercise. But I want to hear about you. How are you really feeling?"

We started the drive home and I told her how I was doing and what the latest news was on my treatment.

"I won't know any results until next week, but I've got my hopes up pretty high. I've heard of so many positive results being achieved with stem cell therapy. And you'll be happy to know I won't be having any more Generator sessions."

"That's a switch. What made you change your mind?" Jasmine asked.

"Partly because I'm part of a control group that won't allow me to be exposed to the Generator while I'm in the stem cell trial. And partly because I've become convinced that the Generator needs further testing."

"I'd like to hear how you came to that conclusion."

"Maybe we can talk about it later. It's a little complicated."

"Okay, I can wait. I've did some reading about stem cell therapy. I'm pretty impressed. And I visited a holistic health clinic in Boulder that an acquaintance told me about. They've had some success using natural treatments for various diseases including malignancy. I brought some information for you to look at."

"Sure, I'll read it. But I'm committed to the stem cell trial for the next month. I'm not sure I want to try and squeeze in a visit to Colorado during that time."

"No, I wasn't suggesting that. But some of the things they recommend can be done on your own. A lot of what they do is related to maximizing your body's immune system with diet and supplements."

"I'm already limiting my sugar intake. I hope I won't have to give up my hamburgers as well," I teased.

"Yum! A hamburger would hit the spot right about now. I forgot how hungry I was. What's for supper?"

"How does grilled steak sound?"

"Can you drive a bit faster? How do you turn off that onboard speed warning thingy?"

"We'll be there in a few minutes. Tell me more about that clinic you visited," I said trying to distract her and keep her mind off food.

———————————————

Monika and Jasmine talked nonstop at supper, and I was content to listen. Afterward we took a long walk. When we got back, I made them some iced tea and we sat down in the family room.

"Dad, I want to hear how you got interested in Christianity. I still find it hard to believe that . . . well, that you believe in God," Jasmine said.

139

I shared a condensed version of my spiritual journey, and after I read verses eight and nine in the second chapter of Ephesians Jasmine asked, "What does 'grace' mean in that verse?"

"My understanding is that it's the opposite of earning something, so it's more like a gift. In this verse it's saying God forgives us and saves us even though we didn't earn it and don't deserve it. Did I tell you my friend, Kharis, chose his nickname from this passage? He told me that the name comes from the Greek word for 'grace.' I'm sure he can explain it better than I can."

"If what you said is true, it goes against what I've learned about other religions. But to be honest, I haven't really studied a lot of them," Jasmine said.

"You'll find that Christianity is unique in that respect. It teaches that God loves us and by sending Jesus to pay the penalty for our sins, he did everything necessary for us to know him and have a relationship with him. We just need to believe and surrender our lives to him."

Jasmine sat quietly for a moment and then said, "I guess I believe that if God does exist, we have to wait until we die to know for sure."

"That's what I thought, too. Now I know he exists and that he loves me. But that's something you have to discover for yourself. I can only help point you in the right direction. The best place to start is to read the Bible and ask God to help you understand it. Ask him if what you're reading is true and if he is real," I said.

"I'm willing to do that. As I've been studying philosophy, I've found lots of truths that I believe in. But I can say that none of them affected me like the Bible seems to have affected you."

"It's the God of the Bible that has affected me. That's much different than trying to apply certain truths or principles to your life."

"I'd like to experience God like you have. I want to discuss this more, but I'm afraid I'm starting to fade. We've got a busy day tomorrow, so I think I should get some sleep."

Monika stood up and said, "Of course. Everything should be ready, but let me know if you need anything. Lori said she'd come at 10:00 tomorrow morning. That means we probably won't see her until 10:30 or so. There's no need for you to get up early."

"I rarely sleep in. Don't worry; I'll be quiet if I get up early. Goodnight." As she walked down the hall, she turned and said, "It's so nice to be home. I miss both of you."

"Goodnight, Jaz. You don't know how wonderful it is to have you here," I said.

"And I feel the same. Goodnight, honey," Monika said.

Chapter 24
Day 64 – Saturday, May 31st

I woke up to the smell of coffee. I put on my robe and went into the kitchen where Jasmine was eating breakfast. She was reading my Bible.

"Good morning, Jaz."

"Good morning, Dad. Hey, do you think the world was created in seven days? I've heard of creationists, but never knew much about what they believed. But that's what it says here in the beginning of the Bible."

"Huh. I haven't read the beginning yet. I started more toward the middle, in the New Testament."

"Why did you do that? You're too methodical to start in the middle of a book."

I tried to explain the difference between the Old Testament and the New Testament with my limited knowledge. "I followed Kharis's advice and started reading in the New Testament. It's mostly about Jesus, and I found it really interesting. Kharis said the Old Testament will make much more sense if you read the New Testament first. I took his word for it. But I've only read a few Psalms, so I don't know much about it yet."

"Genesis seems pretty interesting to me. It goes against everything I've been taught in school. Why didn't they at least tell us there is more than one theory to explain how we got here? Aren't we supposed to be taught how to think and analyze things for ourselves? I want to read more."

"Now you've got me interested. I wish I had more time . . ." I started to say then caught myself. Jasmine looked at me and got tears in her eyes.

"You've got to get better, Dad. I know you will. I've heard that stem cell therapy is almost miraculous. It will work for you. It has to."

"We'll see. Let's not think about that today. I'm getting married tomorrow and I feel like celebrating all weekend. Let's drive to Hampshire Park for a walk. I'll see if Monika wants to join us."

"Yes, let's go. We haven't been on a walk there for years. I'll be ready in a few minutes," she said as she stood up.

Monika decided to stay home. She said she had too many things on her mind and wanted to make sure everything was ready for the wedding. I felt a little guilty when she said that. She looked at me and saw I was hesitant. "It looks like a beautiful day. Go and enjoy some time alone with Jasmine. As long as you're home by 10:00, I'll be happy," she said giving me a kiss and a gentle push out of the bedroom.

As I walked out I said, "That's one thing I love about you. You can read my thoughts—and let me have my way most of the time."

"Don't worry, I'm keeping score. Wait until you hear where I want to go on our honeymoon," she said as she closed the door behind me.

Jasmine and I walked and talked for almost two hours. We covered topics from the trivial to the profound. I felt like we had barely begun to discuss everything that was on her mind—and on mine. As we drove home she told me about James, the latest man in her life.

"He's an amazing person. Maybe we don't have a lot in common, but he's very considerate and kind. He's a pretty fair musician and is learning to compose his own material. But so far he isn't making a living at it."

"How long have you known each other?"

"Three months. He just asked if he could move in with me."

I wasn't sure what to say in response. Jasmine had already lived with two other men and ended up getting hurt both times. I thought she should take things more slowly. I was also surprised to feel a twinge of sadness at the thought of her living with a man. I hadn't felt that in the past.

"What do you think?" I asked.

She thought about it for a moment and then said, "I'm happy with my life. I like my job; I have some good friends; I love the mountains."

"And what about James?" I questioned.

"I have feelings for him. When I moved to Colorado I had a dream of meeting someone, falling in love, and spending my life with him. I thought that would make me the most happy. It hasn't worked out that way."

"No. You've had a couple of tough break-ups. It hurt me to see how much pain it caused you."

"I'm old enough to understand that there's pain in life. It's not that I'm afraid of being hurt again. It's something more than that."

"Are we talking about your decision to live together with James?"

"No. I've been thinking that some man would make me happy. I'm only 22, but I've pretty much given up on that idea. Oh, I'm sure there's happiness to be found in a loving relationship, but I know now that it isn't enough. There must be more."

Inside I was feeling that unexplainable joy that I had become familiar with. I knew exactly what Jasmine was missing—and what I had missed all my life. Only God's love could totally satisfy our inner longings. Looking back I could see that I had resigned myself to 'normal' life shortly after Anne and I started living together. Get established in a career, buy a house, raise some children, a few pleasures and good times here and there—that was all I expected out of life. The inner longings eventually faded, or were crowded out by the ordinary, everyday matters of life, and only occasionally was my mind occupied with more transcendent thought. Jasmine was still searching for deeper meaning to life. There was nothing more I wanted than for her to know Jesus and the fullness of life he provides.

"Jaz, there is more. Much more. God created us to know him and to find our happiness in a relationship with him. When I believed in Jesus I experienced a change inside that is hard to put into words. I used to think like you did when I was younger, but for some reason I stopped searching for a deeper meaning to life. Then when I believed in Jesus I knew that I had found what I had given up trying to find. There is a verse in the Gospel of John that I memorized. Jesus said, 'I am the bread of life. Whoever comes to me will never be hungry again. Whoever believes in me will never be thirsty.' My heart, or my soul, or whatever it is you want to call that inner self, was satisfied—and it still is."

Jasmine looked thoughtful. "I want that, too. The religions and philosophies I've studied so far haven't satisfied me at all. I'm going to look into Christianity."

As I parked the car in the driveway and turned off the engine, I looked at her and asked, "Will you let me go on that journey with you?"

"I could use a good traveling companion. And just think of the endless discussions we can have. Now we need to figure out how to make that work."

"We better do that later. Lori's already here and we've got a full day ahead of us."

Jasmine didn't recognize Lori's car in the street when we drove in. She got excited, jumped out of the car, and ran in the house to see her sister. I took a moment to thank God for one of the best mornings I could remember in a long time, and to pray for Jasmine, and Lori, as well. Whether I lived or died, I decided that the most important thing in my life was to do what I could to see my kids, and Monika, come to know God.

The ladies took over and had the house looking like a wedding chapel by late afternoon. Monika sent me on an errand—probably to get me out of the way—but I was glad to do something to contribute. Besides there was nonstop conversation going on between the three of them, and I didn't mind escaping the commotion for a couple of hours.

We ordered pizza for dinner and ate out on the patio. It was just like old times having the family together, and I enjoyed every minute of it. As we were finishing off the last piece of pizza, someone was at the front door. It was Kharis.

"Evening, Dave. Am I interrupting anything?" he asked.

"Hi, Kharis. We've just finished supper. Come on in and join us for dessert," I said.

He came in and looked around. "Wow! Someone here knows how to decorate."

"Most of it is the handiwork of my daughter, Lori. She wanted to be a fashion designer when she was younger. Come out back and meet her and my other daughter."

We walked out to the patio and I introduced Kharis to Lori and Jasmine. Kharis shook their hands and I noticed his handshake with Jasmine lingered a second or two longer.

"You're the guy who gave my dad a Bible. It sure changed his life. I'm going to give it a try, too," Jasmine said.

Kharis took off his backpack, reached inside, and pulled out a Bible. "Would you accept one from me?" he asked.

Jasmine hesitated a second, then reached out and took it from him. "Thanks so much. I've already started reading Genesis in Dad's Bible. Now we won't have to fight over it."

"Genesis is a great book. You might want to read some from the New Testament at the same time. I'd recommend 'John's Report,' one of the books about the life of Jesus," Kharis said.

"Mom usually reads four or five books at the same time, so I can probably manage two. I'll give it a go," Jasmine said.

Monika and Lori started clearing the plates and Monika said, "You'll have some dessert with us, won't you, Kharis? It's just vanilla ice cream, but we've got fresh strawberries to put on top."

"Thanks. That sounds really good. I'd love some," he answered. Jasmine went to help them prepare the dessert, so Kharis and I were left alone.

"I came by to let you know that Proxy has made a deal with Guardian Security. They want to put their plan into action early next week if they can get everything in place. The only possible glitch is that Guardian Security will need a court order to conduct covert operations with Future Health's security department."

"What are the chances of getting one?"

"Guardian Security said that the log entry together with the Generator data would be sufficient to substantiate our request for a court order. But since the log entry was obtained illegally, the request is going to need the approval of one of Guardian Security's bureau chiefs."

"What's the likelihood of getting that level of approval?"

"That's were Justin comes in. He's willing to use his influence in Guardian Security's D.C. office to get the necessary signatures. In return he's asking for immunity for himself and for Proxy."

"Did Guardian Security agree to those terms?"

"They did. Austin, a Guardian Security agent, has done a good job of convincing his superiors that this is a low-risk operation with potentially great returns. Proxy had a long discussion with Austin and apparently he's intrigued by the evidence we've produced. He confided to Proxy that he's eager to take on a big medical firm that is seemingly flaunting its power with no regard for the public's well-being."

Jasmine was stepping out onto the patio with a tray of ice cream and heard that last remark.

"What was that? Are you two having a discussion about corporate abuse without me? What did I miss?" she said.

Kharis looked at Jasmine, then at me, then at Jasmine again. Maybe I was imagining something, but when he looked at Jasmine the second time I couldn't help but notice how steady his gaze was.

"Jaz, there are a few things I need to explain to you and Lori. I think this is probably the right time. Kharis, do you have any objections?" I asked.

Kharis looked at me and didn't say anything. Finally he spoke. "I trust your judgment. But it would be best not to identify those who aren't here to speak for themselves."

"Of course. I'll be discreet," I said.

"Okay, this sounds like you two are secret agents or something. This better be good. I have a feeling it will be. Lori, Monika, come out here and please hurry," Jasmine said and quickly sat down at the table.

It took quite a while to share the story with them. Jasmine was hanging on every word. Lori appeared to be in a state of shock. I could tell that Monika was relieved that we were finally letting them in on our big secret. When I got to the part where Kharis received the Generator treatment that was meant for me, Lori gasped. Jasmine sat there quietly looking at Kharis. It was clear that he was feeling uncomfortable.

Lori said, "Kharis, if you're that sure the Generator can cause malignancy, isn't there a chance you could get it? Weren't you risking your life?"

"I believed it was something I was supposed to do, that's all," Kharis replied.

"That was a brave thing to do," Jasmine said.

Kharis blushed and didn't say anything. I finished the story and asked Kharis to share the latest news. When he finished I said, "So, your old dad leads a much more exciting life than I'm sure you ever imagined. Wait until you hear the part about the high speed car chase we were in."

Lori blurted out, "Really! Were you driving? Did they catch you?"

Jasmine touched her arm and said, "Lori, you always were a sucker for Dad's lame humor. He's pulling your leg."

Lori sighed then sat back in her chair and said, "I knew that. I was just playing along."

"Right. Like you always do," Jasmine said and they laughed together.

"So Kharis, what do we do now?" I asked.

"Relax and enjoy your wedding. If the request for a court order is granted, I'll contact you. Guardian Security plans to use you, that is, pretend to use you, as bait for catching Future Health in the act. They'll coordinate the operation with the clinic and I imagine they'll inform your doctor of what's going on. Looks like you two might have a lot to talk about at your next appointment."

"Great. I can't wait," I said sarcastically. "Isn't there some way to avoid informing him?"

"Not with Guardian Security involved. We have to play by their rules now," Kharis replied.

"Okay. I'll take it a day at a time. I'm going to put it out of my mind for the next couple of days. Monika, if I bring it up, give me an elbow in the ribs."

"You can count on it. Can you and Lori help me with a couple of final arrangements inside?" Monika said.

I looked at her. She wanted Jasmine and Kharis to be left alone. So she saw something in the way they looked at each other, too. Lori gave a quick glance to Jasmine and then to Monika and understood. She got up and said, "Sure. Come on, Dad; let's finish setting up the dining room."

Jasmine looked surprised and said, "I thought everything was done. What do you want me to do?"

Monika said, "It will just take a few minutes. You entertain Kharis and I'll make some coffee."

Jasmine looked at her mom and her expression told me that she understood what was going on, but she knew she was helpless to do anything about it.

"Okay. But call me if you need me," Jasmine said.

We left them alone for 15 or 20 minutes and then came out with the coffee. Kharis was telling Jasmine how he had become a believer, and she was giving him her full attention.

"Dad, have you heard this story? It's fascinating," Jasmine said.

Lori spoke up, "Dad, you still haven't told us how you became a Christian. I'd like to hear about that. I can't really put my finger on it, but you're different in some way. I mean in a good way."

"I talked to Jaz about it already, so let me give you a quick summary of how it happened." I briefly shared how I had become a believer and then said, "Not only did God forgive me, but he's changing me. I don't understand much yet, but it feels like he is rearranging things inside of me: my priorities, my thoughts, my desires."

Lori spoke first, "That's cool, Dad. But I don't understand what you did that had to be forgiven. You've always been a good person. You've never done anything wrong."

"My whole life I ignored God and never honored him the way I should have. That was my biggest crime. But in my thoughts, words, and actions, I have to admit that I've broken most of God's laws. It wasn't until I started reading the Bible that I understood how much selfishness and pride there really is in my heart. I needed a lot of mercy—and still do!" I said.

Lori said, "Maybe I should try reading the Bible, too. I've done a lot worse things in my life than you have. I guess I need to be forgiven as well."

"You can take my Bible home with you if you want. I'll pick up another one or read Monika's."

Kharis reached for his backpack and pulled out a Bible. "I've got one here that I'd be glad to give to you."

"Thanks so much. I'll be happy to accept it, but I'm afraid I've never been very good at reading actual books. I think I should buy a digital version like Mom's," Lori said.

Kharis pulled out his MiNDi and said, "It just so happens I have a free, public domain version that I can put on your MiNDi in less than a minute. Interested?"

Lori and Jasmine both pulled out their MiNDis at the same time and took him up on his offer. Then I reached for mine.

Chapter 25

Day 63 – Sunday, June 1st

Monika woke up early and started getting breakfast ready. Jasmine was helping her when I came into the kitchen.

"Dad! Look at that sunshine. We can have the ceremony on the patio. Let's move the flowers out right after breakfast. And we need to set up some chairs and put a table out there," she said excitedly.

"Whoa! I haven't had my coffee yet. There's plenty of time. We should wait a couple of hours to make sure it isn't going to rain," I said.

"Rain! Look at that sky. It's not going to rain. The weather is perfect."

"We should wait a couple of hours until I'm really awake and feel like doing any physical labor," I said.

"You could have said that in the first place. Okay, we can wait—but not two hours!"

We sat down to breakfast and Jasmine said, "What's the idea leaving me alone with Kharis last night? That was a little too obvious to me, and I'm sure it was to him, as well. He's a nice guy though. He must be seeing someone." I gave Monika a quick glance; she understood and we pretended to ignore Jasmine.

"Well, is he or isn't he?" Jasmine said with a slightly annoyed tone of voice.

Monika and I laughed. "He is seeing someone, but I don't know if it's serious," I said.

"What about your latest heart-throb?" Monika asked.

"Infatuation is more like it. He's a cool guy and he treats me well, but I've been thinking more along the lines of a long-term relationship, and I don't think he's the one for that."

"I'm glad to hear you're giving it some careful thought," Monika commented. "I'm sorry if we put you on the spot last night. But I like Kharis and I thought you two might hit it off. But we know you're old enough to make your own decisions about who you're interested in and who is just interesting. He's certainly the latter."

"Yes, he is. I have a hundred questions I would have liked to bring up last night. Oh well, I'm leaving on Wednesday. I won't get the opportunity."

"How about I try and arrange for him to come by before you leave?" I suggested.

"I wouldn't object. But it can't interfere with our Tuesday plans. I'm looking forward to spending most of the day with the two of you," Jasmine responded.

"I'll see what I can do," I said.

Lori arrived after breakfast and then Monika's sister, Emily, came. I hadn't seen her since I was diagnosed with malignancy.

"Hello, Emily. Good to see you," I said.

"Dave, forgive me for not coming to see you sooner. Monika's been keeping me up-to-date on how you're doing. You look marvelous. How are you feeling?"

"I'd say pretty normal. It's hard to believe that I'm really sick. Come in and sit down. Have a cup of coffee before Lori puts you to work."

Just then Jasmine walked in from the patio and screamed, "Aunt Emmy! I've missed you!" She ran over to Emily and gave her a long hug.

"Jasmine, you're as skinny as a rail. And look at your hair! I bet you haven't cut it since I saw you last," Emily said. Lori came over and hugged Emily, then Monika came in and they all started talking at once. I was badly outnumbered. I listened politely for several minutes and then slipped out onto the porch. Lori came looking for me an hour later.

"Hiding as usual I see. It's okay to come in now. Everyone is busy and we need your help on the patio," she said.

An hour later everything was ready to go. The caterer showed up and the ladies started organizing the food.

We all sat down and had a snack and then it was time for Monika to start getting dressed for the ceremony. Owen and Amelia arrived at 12:45 and right behind them the judge came walking up.

We were ready for Monika to make her appearance at 1:00. Lori started the music and a couple minutes later Monika came out of the bedroom. She was glowing, and looked beautiful in her dress and holding the bouquet Lori had made for her. The ceremony was brief and the judge asked if we wanted to say anything before he pronounced us man and wife. Monika and I had discussed it beforehand and decided to keep our vows brief.

We turned and looked at each other, then Monika said, "Dave, after all these years, I know that our feelings for one another can ebb and flow, and that they can't be the basis for a life-long relationship. Love is a choice and involves commitment. So I promise to love and respect you. No matter what the future might hold, I will stay by your side for the rest of my life."

Then I said to Monika, "Monika, in the book of Ephesians it says that I should love you just like Christ loved the church and gave his life for it. By God's grace, I'm going to try and do that. I promise to love you and put your needs before my own. I'm asking God to show me how to be the kind of husband he wants me to be. In all that I do, I want to Jesus to be honored and to have first place."

We turned to face the judge and he pronounced us man and wife. We kissed and everyone applauded. Monika asked the ladies to come forward. Then she turned and threw the bouquet of flowers over her shoulder. It went over Jasmine's outstretched arm right into the hands of Amelia. She laughed and turned to look at Owen. He looked horrified and shot a meaningful glance at me. I laughed, but Owen didn't seem particularly amused. Fortunately everyone starting coming up to congratulate us at that point, and Owen appeared to be off the hook.

The other guests started arriving at 2:00. Everyone except Proxy was able to come. Kharis came by himself, and at one point I noticed that he and Jasmine were alone talking together. The crowd was small enough that I was able to relax and enjoy myself.

I had time to visit with everyone. I could see that Monika was excited and thoroughly enjoying herself. It was almost 5:00 by the time the last guests left. Lori and Caleb stayed to help clean up. Around 8:00 I told them to go home and get some rest.

"Okay, we'll go, but I'm coming back tomorrow morning to finish."

"Don't you have to work?" I asked.

"I took the day off so I could help, and so I could spend some time with Jasmine. Maybe we'll even have time to get in some shopping," Lori said. Monika and Jasmine looked at each other and groaned. "Well, we need to at least go to a nice restaurant," Lori said sounding a little disappointed.

Monika said, "Now you're talking. I'll make reservations for 1:00 for the three of us. Now you two go home and get some rest. We've still got a lot to do tomorrow morning."

Lori and Caleb left, and then I collapsed into a chair. I realized that we hadn't eaten since mid-afternoon, so we all raided the refrigerator and brought our food into living room. We ate and talked about how well everything went, and what a good time we had.

After an hour or so, Jasmine and Monika got up and took the plates into the kitchen. While they were cleaning up, I stretched out on the couch. The next thing I remember was waking up in the middle of the night and making my way to the bedroom.

Chapter 26
Day 62 – Monday, June 2nd

I felt bad leaving for work on Monday morning knowing that I was leaving Monika, Lori, and Jasmine to finish cleaning up after the wedding. But they didn't seem to mind, and they promised that they would stop working by 12:00 whether they were done or not, and take the afternoon off to do something fun.

I had almost finished putting together the transition plan, and I wanted it to be ready to give to Julia on Wednesday. I was still optimistic about overcoming malignancy and keeping my job, but I needed to be prepared for the worst. If someone would be stepping into my position in a month, I didn't want them to face some of the challenges I did when I first started.

My plan was to take off Tuesday afternoon to spend time with Jasmine, so I ate lunch at my desk and worked right through the afternoon without a break. By 5:00 I felt good about the progress I had made. I was on my way home when Hailey announced, "Call from Ms. Moreno. Connect?"

"Connect. Hello, Ms. Moreno," I said.

"Hello, Mr. Roberts. There's some news to report about our case. Would you be able to stop by the office anytime soon?"

"How about in 20 minutes?"

"Excellent. I'll see you then."

I hoped it wouldn't take long. I wanted to enjoy the evening with Monika and Jasmine, and they were expecting me by 6:00. If I was in and out of the law office in 15 minutes, I could make it home on time.

When I stepped into Maria's office, I saw Kharis was there.

Maria said, "Hi, Dave. Thanks for coming. I'm sure you want to get home to spend time with your lovely daughters and your beautiful bride. I really enjoyed being at your wedding and meeting them."

"I'm glad you could come. Lori won't be there tonight, but I would like to get home as quickly as possible."

"Kharis came by an hour ago with news from Max. Thanks to Justin's efforts in D.C., the judge granted Guardian Security the court order. They've already made arrangements with the manager of security at Future Health to conduct a surveillance operation and to place an agent on site. Tomorrow morning someone from Guardian Security will visit the health clinic and meet with the administrator. The plan is to schedule the sting operation for Wednesday morning."

"That's good news and I'm glad to know what's going on. But couldn't you have waited to contact me?" I asked.

"We wanted you to know that tomorrow your doctor will be told about the sting operation. Guardian Security is going to schedule a fake Generator session for you and that means your doctor must be informed. I'm sure he'll have some questions for you. When you talk to him, we'd prefer that you not identify any of us by name," Maria said.

"Kharis said this might happen. So how much will he be told?" I asked.

"As I understand, he'll be told that the cyber attack last week was related to the current investigation, and that it appears someone is attempting to tamper with the Generator formulas," Maria replied. "He'll also be informed that you were specifically targeted on previous occasions, and that's why Guardian Security will be using you to lure them into their trap."

"Okay, I can understand why you wanted to talk to me. I'll be prepared for my doctor's call. Is that it for now?"

"Yes, that's everything," Maria replied.

I stood up and said, "I'd like to observe when they conduct the operation. Can you find out if that's possible?"

Kharis responded, "I'll find out. I can come by your house tomorrow and let you know what's going on."

"I won't be home until 7:30 tomorrow evening. I've got a date with Jasmine and Monika."

"She leaves town on Wednesday morning, right?" Kharis asked.

"That's right," I replied.

"I'd like to talk to her before she leaves," Kharis said.

"She'll be there tomorrow night. I'll tell her you're coming by. Anything special you want to talk to her about if you don't mind my asking?"

"I'd like to stay in touch with her if she's interested," Kharis said.

"What about your girlfriend?" I asked.

"To be honest, we haven't been seeing each other very long and neither of us has much emotional energy invested in the relationship. She's just been too busy with her studies, and I've been busy with CAGE," Kharis answered.

"Sorry for prying. You two are adults and it's not my place to meddle." As I walked to the door I gave Kharis a small wink and said, "But I'll put in a good word for you."

Maria said, "This could be an eventful week. I'm letting Kharis use my car and I'm going to use a company car. And remember, CAGE is still under investigation so let's continue to be careful in all of our electronic communications."

"Sure. I'll be careful," I said. "See you tomorrow, Kharis."

"I'll plan on coming by around 8:00," Kharis said.

I took a few steps down the hall then turned back and said, "Kharis, you didn't hear it from me, but Jasmine isn't particularly fond of facial hair, or long hair for that matter."

"Ouch! I haven't shaved in six years," he said stroking his beard.

"Looks like you haven't visited a barber in that long, either," I said with a smile.

I made it home on time and we all sat down to dinner. Jasmine wanted to know what I learned from Maria. I updated her on the situation and told her that Kharis would be stopping by Tuesday evening with the latest news. She seemed pleased.

"Do you think he'll have time to discuss a few questions?" she asked.

"I imagine so. He has a question or two for you, as well," I said.

"He does?" she said.

"Just so you'll be prepared, he wants to stay in touch with you after you leave. I think he's interested in you, so if it's not mutual, I'd recommend being honest with him,"

Jasmine said, "Thanks for letting me know. And you know that I'll be totally honest with him. I never play games in relationships."

"Sorry. I didn't need to say that. You know how to handle yourself. So, what are you going to say to him?" I asked.

She thought about that and then answered, "I'm going to say that I'd like to keep in touch."

Chapter 27
Day 61 – Tuesday, June 3rd

As soon as I got to work I had my regular meeting with my assistant managers. As we finished up, I reminded them that I had scheduled a full departmental meeting for Friday. That was when I would break the news to everyone that I had malignancy and would be leaving UBC in a month.

I left the office at 12:00. Monika and Jasmine were ready to go when I got home. I went up and changed, they packed the car, and we were on our way. We drove to one of our favorite hiking spots on the river. After about an hour hike we arrived at the waterfall and sat down to have lunch. As we sat enjoying the view, we reminisced about some of the good times we had over the years. The sun was dancing on the river and the sound of the water rushing over the rocks was music to my ears. A thought came into my head during one of the lulls in our conversation: someday I'd like to bring my grandchildren here. It was a sad to think that day might never come, but my view of life was changing, maybe because of my faith, or maybe because I had to deal with the possibility of dying. I could enjoy this day and whatever tomorrow might bring. I didn't need to worry or be afraid. I was thankful to be here with two people I loved.

After the hike we decided to rent a canoe and paddle around on the river for a while. I had brought my fishing gear and Jasmine sat in the front of the canoe and tried her luck. It was a little cool out on the water so after an hour we headed to shore. We stopped and had dinner on the drive back and arrived home just before 7:30. I was tired and decided to rest before Kharis arrived. Jasmine went to shower and Monika made some coffee.

Kharis arrived promptly at 8:00. I invited him in and he said, "Hello, Dave. Whoa, you look a little red. Does it hurt?"

Now that he mentioned it, I did feel a little sunburned. I didn't realize I had gotten that much sun. I answered him, "Just a little. Come on in and I'll call the ladies. Do you want something to drink? Monika just made coffee."

"No, thanks; not right now."

Monika and Jasmine joined us and we all sat down.

"Everything is all set. Guardian Security told the clinic to schedule a Generator appointment for you for tomorrow morning. Someone spoke to your doctor, so he's aware of what's happening. Proxy asked the Guardian Security agent if you could be present when they run the trace. They said you can, but that there really isn't much to it. Once they know which computer at Future Health is being used, their agent on site at Future Health will take over. Not very exciting," Kharis said.

"No, I guess not. And I'll be taking Jasmine to the airport in the morning, so I can't be there regardless. Will Proxy be observing?" I asked.

"Both of us will be at the Guardian Security office downtown. You can stop by on the way back from the airport, and we can tell you what they found," Kharis suggested.

"Okay, I should be there by noon or shortly after. I'm really anxious to find out how Future Health will react when Guardian Security closes in."

"They'll call their lawyers, that's all. Don't expect any admission of guilt or explanations," Jasmine said.

Kharis nodded in agreement. "She's right. It will be completely boring—until the press gets a hold of it."

"Do you think they'll be informed?" Monika asked.

"If all goes as planned, then Guardian Security is going to blow their own trumpet as loud as they can. That's probably why they agreed to Proxy's demands in the first place. They'll get plenty of positive and free PR," Kharis responded.

"Good. Get the public up in arms and some semblance of justice might be administered. But you can forget about true justice or restitution. If they've caused harm to thousands of people, no amount of money could compensate the victims or their families," Jasmine said.

"First things first," I said. "It won't be easy determining who is really to blame—even with Guardian Security using all their modern electronic surveillance technology. I'll be satisfied to see something is done to make sure no more people are harmed by the Generator."

Kharis echoed my sentiment, "That's what I want more than anything. I'd be happy to work myself out of a job."

"You're already out of a job," I reminded him.

"That's a true statement," Kharis said with a grin.

"Any developments in the CAGE saga?" Monika asked.

Kharis answered, "Lots of lawyers and lots of talking. I think the government's case against us is weak, but they are forcing us to use our time and resources to fight their charges. That may be all they're after. There's talk of dissolving CAGE and reorganizing, but that will take weeks. Maria knows more about what's happening, but I've been too busy to discuss it with her lately."

"Maybe you'll have more free time on your hands soon," I said. "Any idea what you'll do when this is resolved?" I asked.

"I'm thinking and praying about that. Proxy says he could help me get started as a computer security consultant just about anywhere. I've learned a lot from him, and he's willing to continue to train me."

"That sounds like a tempting offer. When the time comes, I can put in a recommendation for you at UBC. They use a lot of computer consultants," I offered.

"Thanks, Dave. I'd appreciate that."

"If you have time, Jasmine has some questions for you, Kharis. I've got a few things to get done for work, so if you'll excuse me and Monika, we'll give you two a little time to talk."

"Sure. I can stay for awhile," Kharis said.

"Maybe you'd like to sit out on the patio. It's a nice evening. Would either of you like anything to drink?" Monika asked.

"I'll take that cup of coffee now," Kharis said as he stood up and walked toward the kitchen. Can I bring you something, Jasmine?"

"Coffee with a little cream, please," she replied.

The two of them went out to the patio and talked. Around 10:00 Jasmine came and told me Kharis had to be going. I went to say goodbye.

"Thanks for coming by, Kharis," I said.

"It was my pleasure. Jasmine asked some pretty deep questions about spiritual matters. I'm not sure I was able to answer them satisfactorily, but I told her I'd be happy to talk to her again anytime. We agreed to talk on a regular basis for the next few weeks."

I was glad to hear that, but I kept my opinion to myself. "Now that you've got so much free time, I've got some questions to discuss with you, too," I said to Kharis.

"Be happy to. But the next couple of days look to be busy. Let's put it off until later in the week," Kharis replied.

"I was thinking the same thing. Maybe this weekend," I suggested.

"Alright. I'll see you tomorrow, Dave. Say goodnight to Monika for me."

"I will. See you tomorrow," I said.

After he left I asked Jasmine how it went.

"I'm not sure. He expressed an interest in getting to know me better, but I'd have to say he came across as cautious. Or maybe he's just shy. We'll see what happens."

"Cautious is okay with me. You do jump into relationships too quickly if you don't mind my saying so."

"Hmm," she said and paused before asking me, "How long was it before you and Monika moved in together?"

"Ouch! You're right. But I have learned a thing or two over the years, and I'm trying to look out for my little girl."

She gave me a hug and said, "And I love you for that. Don't worry; I'm going to take it more slowly next time."

"You must be exhausted. I know I am. I'm going to turn in," I said.

"All that fresh air and sun took its toll on me, too. Sleep well. I love you, Dad."

"I love you, Jasmine. I wish you weren't leaving tomorrow."

"I know. It was way too short of a visit."

"If I recover, I hope to come see you this summer. But we can talk about that later."

Jasmine looked at me for several seconds and said, "We'll see each other again soon, I promise."

Chapter 28
Day 60 – Wednesday, June 4th

Lori surprised us by coming over early to say goodbye to Jasmine. We all had breakfast together and before we knew it, it was time to leave for the airport. After some quick hugs and goodbyes, Jasmine and I were on our way. The conversation was pretty light-hearted and upbeat, which I was thankful for. I was feeling emotional about saying goodbye, and I didn't want to have time to think about it. We parked and I walked with Jasmine to the terminal.

"I didn't ask about your spiritual discussion with Kharis last night. Was it useful?" I asked.

"I've got a lot to think about. I've never met anyone like him. The thing that struck me in our conversation is that he mostly talks about his relationship with Jesus, not about religion or philosophy. He said that he thought I was a truth seeker, and he encouraged me not to give up on my quest. He read a verse about Jesus coming to give us abundant life, and that true joy and happiness could only be found in him. I really liked that. I think I've become aware of something missing in my life. If Jesus is the answer, then that empty feeling should go away if I believe in him."

"It worked that way for me. Keep searching, and I'll be here to help in any way I can. As Kharis told me, God is not trying to hide himself from us. If we sincerely seek him, he'll reveal himself to us."

"He told me something similar. It was reassuring."

We arrived at the ticket counter and couldn't continue our conversation. Then we walked over to the security check and it was time to say goodbye. We both shed a few tears as we hugged each other, but I felt more happy than sad.

"I'll be praying for you, Jaz," I said.

"Thanks, Dad."

"Call us when you arrive."

"I will. I'm anxious to hear what happens today."

I stayed and watched until she made it through security. Then she waved and headed toward the gate. I looked at my watch; it was almost noon. I walked to the car and headed downtown. Thirty minutes later I was walking into the main office of Guardian Security. They called someone to escort me to a room where I saw Proxy and Kharis, and some Guardian Security agents.

Walking over to me Kharis said, "Dave, you're just in time."

"What happened?" I asked.

Kharis responded, "It went as planned. When the Generator session was initiated at 10:30, Guardian Security detected another computer accessing the Generator across the Net. They traced it to a computer at Future Health that's located in the accounting department. When the Guardian Security agent closed in, there was nobody using it. They confiscated the computer and are bringing it to their Atlanta headquarters. Future Health is up-in-arms. Their lawyers are already on alert."

"So what now? Do they have a suspect?"

"No, they don't. Proxy said it was most likely a bot program and now the difficult part will be finding out who controls it."

"What's a bot program?"

"A program that is installed on the computer and runs either automatically or by someone from another computer who sends it commands. In this case Guardian Security was able to determine that nobody had connected to that computer across the Net this morning, so it had to be running automatically."

"I'm not sure I understand how that all works, but don't bother trying to explain it. How do we catch the criminals?" I asked.

"Now that the computer has been disconnected from the Net, I'm not sure. If they had left it alone, Guardian Security could have monitored it and that might have led us to the guilty party. I hope they know what they are doing," Kharis said.

I was frustrated. "You mean they could have bungled the operation?"

"It's possible, but we have to give them the benefit of the doubt. Let's see what they plan to do."

We walked into an adjoining room. Proxy was there pacing back and forth and visibly agitated. There were two agents working together at one computer; another agent was talking to someone on the phone. When Proxy saw us, he came over.

"If they blew it, I'm going to the press with two good stories! I can't believe they didn't take my advice. When we found out the computer was in the accounting department, I warned them not to touch it. If the person behind this hasn't already been tipped off, he will be when he tries to access the missing computer."

"So where does that leave us?" I asked.

"Ask them?" Proxy said nodding toward the agents.

We watched and waited for an opportunity to talk to them. One of the agents noticed us looking at her, but she ignored us. After several minutes she smiled at us and motioned for us to come over. We walked up to her.

"Gentlemen, you were right. Someone has very cleverly been able to run a program undetected from within Future Health's computer network. Our Atlanta office is analyzing the computer and will update us when they know more. But we know that it was running automatically and that it had access to a computer in the R&D department where experimental Generator formulas were stored."

Proxy smirked, "That's not much new information. We need to find out who is responsible, and you've probably ruined our chances to find out who that is."

The agent stayed calm and said, "There's more than one way to catch the criminal. We're already investigating several possible suspects. And we can be pretty sure there is an inside person involved. The Generator wasn't hacked into; the access codes were used to get to it."

I could see that Proxy calmed down a little. Apparently, he was thinking about what she said.

"There can't be too many people who have authority to use the Generator access codes, or to find out what they are," Proxy said.

"Right. We've already begun tracking down those people. That limits the number of suspects considerably," the agent said.

"We're also looking for a potential money trail, and we're looking at anyone who might have a score to settle with Future Health," the agent responded.

"How long will all that take?" I asked.

The agent shook her head, "I can't say, but I'd recommend you all go home. We'll contact you when we have something."

Proxy folded his arms across his chest and said, "I'm staying put. There must be something I can do to help."

"I'm staying as well," Kharis added.

The agent sighed and said, "I'll see if I can find anything for you to do."

I would have liked to stay, but I had to get to the office and finish preparing for the meeting on Friday. And I wanted to personally notify HR of my M-60 status. Besides, there wasn't any point in hanging around. I couldn't do anything useful to help out.

"I'm going to go to the office. Call me right away if you learn anything, Kharis," I said.

"I will. I'll call later to update you even if we don't make any progress," Kharis said.

"Thanks. I'd appreciate that," I said and left.

When I got to the office I walked by Julia's office. She was there, but on a call. She saw me and motioned to let me know she'd stop by when she finished.

I went to my office and sat at my desk. I sat there quietly for a few minutes gazing at some of the personal things that I had placed around my office. It was strange to think that in a few weeks I would have to pack up and move out. Over and over I had hoped there would be a way to avoid this. I wanted to keep my job, and I didn't feel like reporting my M-60 status to HR. But I had no choice. I wasn't angry about it. This was a comfortable and familiar place, and I realized that the thought of giving it up and facing the unknown scared me. I knew what my response to fear should be; I prayed. Then I remembered Jesus' words when he called his disciples: "Follow me." What was I afraid of? I was following Jesus. I stood up and said to myself, "It's time. This is in your hands now, God."

I walked out of my office and headed downstairs. I went up to Laura in HR and said, "Hi, Laura. How are you doing?"

"Hi, Dave. I'm fine. What brings you down here today?"

"Unfortunately I'm here to let you know that today I'm M-60. Will you update my personnel file for me?"

She looked stunned and seemed uncomfortable. She stammered, "What? Yes, of course. I can take care of it. I'm so sorry." She turned to her monitor and seemed flustered, and then she sighed and stood up.

"Dave, this is a shock. I don't know what to say. What does the doctor think about your chances?"

"I'm participating in a clinical trial for stem cell transplants, and they've been having some success with the treatment. I had my first transplant last week and tomorrow I should find out if I've made any progress. I'm hopeful."

"That sounds encouraging. You look fine. Are you feeling alright?"

"Other than a little fatigue now and then, I feel normal."

"So you have a doctor's appointment tomorrow? If you have a chance, will you please let me know how it went?"

"Sure. Thanks for your concern. And you'll take care of updating my file, right?"

"Don't worry; I'll take it from here."

I went back to my office. I felt relieved to have that behind me, but a little unsettled. If I survived, what did the future hold for me? I sat down and looked at the pile of work on my desk. I had one month left with UBC. I had taken a lot of time off over the last few weeks, and I hadn't kept up on my work the way I should have. It was time to dig in and finish strong. The transition plan was nearly ready. I had started putting together a proposal for restructuring our customer service operations, but so far it was a jumble of incomplete thoughts and ideas. In the next few weeks I needed to use my skills and experience to put them together into a coherent form. I wouldn't have time to complete a detailed plan, but I could make a good start at one. I felt unusually motivated and got right to work.

Julia stopped by in the afternoon and I updated her on what had happened that morning. She listened intently and when I finished she said, "Someone has a lot to answer for. Thousands of people suffered and maybe died. And for what? Does Guardian Security have any idea why someone would do something like this?"

"Just theories at this point. One idea is that someone at Future Health is experimenting with new formulas to try and find a cure for malignancy. Unfortunately, he or she doesn't care how much human suffering they might inflict in the process," I replied.

Julia sighed. "That's depressing. I makes me feel tired of . . ." She didn't finish her thought. "My brother's life was turned upside down when he lost his wife to malignancy. It's hard to believe that someone could be so depraved and self-serving to deliberately cause such misery and pain."

"We still don't know for sure who's behind this or why they're doing it. Whether or not the people responsible are caught, there will be an investigation into the Generator. I trust that the problems will be corrected and the abuse stopped."

"Yes, I'm sure you're right. That's something to be thankful for. And you had a big part in making that happen."

"No, I didn't. But I did have a small role to play. Maybe it was part of God's plan for my life."

"I've known you for years, Dave, and never heard you speak about God before," Julia commented.

"I became a Christian recently," I said.

"That's wonderful! I'd like to hear more about that sometime."

"Sure, I'd love to tell you my story. By the way, I wanted to let you know that I just spoke to Laura in HR and notified her of my M-60 status."

"I've been dreading this day. This mandatory notification law is just not right. Have you contacted anyone yet about filing a discrimination lawsuit?"

"I put in a call. But I haven't had time to meet with anyone or fill out the forms they require. There's been too much going on in my life."

"That's an understatement. So when will you find out if the stem cell therapy is helping?"

"I should know something tomorrow or the next day. I have a second transplant and an MRI scheduled in the morning."

"As soon as you find out something, please let me know."

"I'll make sure you're one of the first to hear."

"Good. I'll see you tomorrow," she said as she got up to leave.

"Thanks, Julia. See you tomorrow."

The rest of the afternoon passed quickly. As I started the drive home I called Monika to see what time she would be done at work. She said she had a few things to finish up, but planned on being home by 6:30. Jasmine had called to let her know that she got home safely.

"We talked for several minutes. She's pretty worried about you. It was hard for her to leave this morning. She's already trying to find a way to get off of work so she can come back," Monika said.

"Thanks for letting me know. I'll call her tonight." The dash monitor was notifying me that Kharis was calling. "Hold on, Monika. I've got to take a call from Kharis."

"I'll let you go. See you at home," she said.

"Okay, I'll see you soon."

I told Hailey to connect me to Kharis.

"Hello, Dave."

"Hello, Kharis. Any news?"

"No breakthrough yet. The Guardian Security D.C. office is sifting through a list of suspects. Proxy is working remotely with the Atlanta team trying to decrypt some files on the computer they confiscated. Future Health sent one of their network security experts to the Guardian Security Atlanta office to help out. I heard that Future Health is willing to cooperate with the investigation in any way they can."

"That's good to hear. And what are you up to?"

"I've been looking through some of Future Health's R&D records. I just uncovered some disturbing information."

"What was that?" I asked anxiously.

"The formula that was used on you—and me—was not some new, experimental formula. It's an old formula that was marked as dangerous and shown to be harmful to healthy cells in their experiments."

That news hit me like a fist in the stomach. As I thought about what it meant, I felt a wave of fear mixed with anger sweep over me. If what Kharis said was true, then someone was not running an unauthorized test of a new Generator formula. The formula was sent to the Generator to deliberately harm me. And quite possibly, the person knew it could infect me with malignancy. How many others had been treated with the same formula? And why?

"Is there any way to verify that?" I asked.

"A Guardian Security agent is doing that now. Future Health is cooperating, so it shouldn't take long. But it's easy to see that the formulas match," Kharis responded.

"Will you be able to see if the same formula was used on others?"

"Proxy said that there is most likely a database on the confiscated computer that will tell us what formulas were used and the names of the people that were treated. But it will probably be a partial list."

"I can't believe it. Why would someone do that?" I asked.

"It's hard to say. Maybe for money, or maybe an act of revenge. But this is so diabolical, we can't rule out the possibility that it could be the work of a psychotic."

"A very intelligent and malevolent one," I added.

"I've got to go; an agent needs to speak with me. Will I be able to reach you later?"

"Yes. I'll be home this evening."

"Okay. I'll call or maybe stop by. See you."

As I drove, I thought about how wrong we had been. We had assumed that experimental formulas were being tested—formulas that might potentially be a cure for malignancy. Yes, it was immoral and illegal to test formulas on unsuspecting patients, and that seemed evil enough. But something good might have come out of it in the end if a cure for malignancy was found. Countless lives might be saved. Now the picture was different. In all likelihood, someone was intentionally trying to infect people with malignancy.

"Why would anyone do that? There must be a reason behind this," I thought. I was no criminologist, but I thought about possible motives: money, revenge, maybe a hate crime of some sort. I was sure that Guardian Security was aware of all of those and was doing what they could to generate a list of suspects.

I got home and Monika wasn't there, so I made myself a sandwich and sat down to watch the news. My mind was elsewhere and I wasn't paying much attention until I heard the announcer say, "Future Health issued a statement this afternoon saying it is temporarily suspending use of the Generator in order to run diagnostic testing on them. They express their regrets and sincere apologies to everyone for this unforeseen interruption of service. In a related story, we have learned that Future Health is being investigated for possible illegal activities in their Research and Development department. There may be a connection between the investigation and the Generator being shutdown, but at this point we can't be sure."

It didn't take long for that news to get out. But the media was obviously wrong about the investigation of Future Health, and I wondered where that information came from. It looked like a case of irresponsible reporting. They didn't mention any of their sources or substantiate their story in any way. Their allegations could seriously damage Future Health's public image. Just then Monika came home.

"Hi, honey. Did I hear right? Is there something on the news about this already?" she asked.

"Future Health has taken the Generator offline for testing. And there are allegations of illegal activity by Future Health's R&D department," I said.

"Do you think they were actually involved?"

"Not after what Kharis found out today," I said and explained what he had discovered.

"I can't believe it. Who could do such a thing? How many people were harmed? And think of all the people who will suffer because they won't be able to receive Generator treatments."

"I'm sure there will be an investigation of it by the Ministry of Health. But there's no telling how long it will take. Cancer patients may need to rely on stem cell therapy again." As I said that, it was as if a light came on. "That could be it!" I said.

"What could be it?" Monika asked.

"What if Nucell is somehow behind this? They were the ones most affected by the success of the Generator. Their company must have lost billions of dollars when stem cell therapy for cancer was superseded by the Generator."

"That's true. But now they are expanding operations because of their success treating malignancy. They've got a corner on that market."

"That's my point. They weren't trying to recapture the market for cancer treatment; they were trying to create a market for their malignancy treatment. And by increasing the number of cases of malignancy, they assure their success."

"I understand your reasoning, but it sounds pretty far-fetched to me. For one thing, think about the risk they would be taking. What if they were caught?"

"Like Proxy said when he thought Future Health was responsible, if they got caught somebody would probably go to jail, but the company would survive. It's a similar case with Nucell. After all, Nucell would have the only effective means of treating malignancy. I'm going to call Kharis."

Kharis was still at the Guardian Security office when I reached him.

"Hello, Dave. I was planning to call you later," he said.

"I know, but I wanted to talk to you right away. We believed that Future Health was trying to find a cure for malignancy, but Nucell has already achieved some level of success treating malignancy with stem cell therapy. They're the ones who stand to profit by increasing the number of malignancy cases. They could be sabotaging the Generator. What do you think?" I asked.

"I think you'd make a good agent. Guardian Security has already considered that possibility. Their computers are analyzing thousands of suspects and mountains of data. You wouldn't believe the amount of information they have available to them. I'm sure you know that they maintain complete records of our electronic footprints, including our Net activity, how we spend our money, and even our whereabouts. They gave me a quick look at my file. Within seconds that can put together a profile that shows the kind of clothes I like to wear, what my favorite foods are, what I like to read, watch, or listen to, and where I'm likely to spend my free time. They know more about me than I do!"

"It's scary, isn't it? The only privacy we have left is in our homes with the blinds closed."

"Assuming you don't use any Net devices," Kharis added wryly.

"I suppose this isn't the time to rant about the death of our right to privacy. So how long is the current list of suspects?" I asked.

"I have no idea. One of the agents is keeping us apprised of the situation, and the last thing she told me was that they're questioning everyone who could possibly access the Generator codes. Unfortunately, the codes weren't secured as tightly as they should have been. Future Health's security chief admitted that they failed to anticipate the possibility of someone stealing the codes in order to send unauthorized formulas to the Generator."

"So the codes could have been easily stolen?" I asked.

"I wouldn't say easily, but yes, they could have been stolen."

"Wonderful. And what about the computer they confiscated? Have they gotten anywhere examining it?"

"Nowhere. Proxy thinks it could take days or weeks to decrypt the files."

"So all we can do is wait?" I asked.

"Yup. It's mostly up to Guardian Security now. I'm going to check in with Proxy and see if there's anything I can help with. I'll give you a call tomorrow morning."

"I've got an appointment at the hospital at 10:00 and won't be done until 12:30 or 1:00."

"Oh, that's right. I hope that goes well. I'll leave a message if you aren't available."

"Thanks. I'll check in with you sometime tomorrow," I said.

Chapter 29
Day 59 – Thursday, June 5th

I had trouble sleeping and got out of bed in the middle of the night to keep from waking Monika. I was laying on the couch thinking and must have finally dozed off, because the next thing I remember was Monika nudging me trying to wake me up.

"It's time to get up. Today's a big day. Did you get any sleep?"

I was groggy. I mumbled, "Not much. Will you get the coffee started? I'll get up in a minute."

"Do you want me to make you breakfast?"

"No. Just coffee. You need to get to work."

The smell of the coffee perking motivated me to crawl off the couch. I joined Monika at the table as she was just finishing her breakfast.

"You'll call me when you finish at the hospital, right?" she asked.

"Yes, I'll call you."

"And you'll call if you find out anything about the investigation?"

"Why don't you just tag along behind me today?" I said with the faintest hint of irritation in my voice.

"I can see you're grumpy. I think I'd rather go to work," she said.

She was right; I was out of sorts. "Sorry. I didn't get enough sleep. I'll do my best to keep you in the loop. Maybe we can eat out tonight or have take-out."

"Sure, it's your turn to cook, so you pick the easy way out," she said as she kissed me and headed for the door.

"Guilty," I said.

"That's okay. But do you remember that after the first transplant you didn't feel like eating? Let's wait and see how it goes today. See you tonight," she said as she walked out the door. A few seconds later she stuck her head back in and said, "I love you. And don't be late for your appointment."

"I won't. I love you, too."

As I ate breakfast I surfed through the news channels and found there was already public reaction about Future Health suspending use of the Generator. People wanted to know how long it would be before the testing was completed, reporters were demanding to know more about the investigation, Future Health's stock had dropped over 12 percent, and not surprisingly, Nucell's stock had risen eight percent. Clearly Nucell stood to profit from any setbacks Future Health would experience from the Generator being taken out of service. What seemed particularly insightful yesterday, seemed quite obvious to me today, and I imagine many others were thinking along the same lines based on the sudden rise in Nucell's stock value.

As I cleaned up the breakfast dishes I continued listening to the news. When I finished I showered and got dressed, and then went into the kitchen to pour myself another cup of coffee. I wanted to call Kharis, but he may have had a late night and I didn't want to risk waking him. I checked for messages and saw that Dr. Steele had called while I was in the shower. I knew why he was calling, and I didn't want to talk to him right now. It could wait until after my appointment. There were a few messages from work that needed my attention, and by the time I finished with them it was time to leave.

On the drive to the hospital I prayed and tried to relax. I was feeling a bit nervous about the injection, but I had already decided not to ask for a tranquilizer so that I would be able to drive afterwards.

I arrived 15 minutes early for my appointment. The receptionist greeted me and sat down at the computer to check me in. Suddenly he stopped. "Please wait here, Mr. Roberts," he said.

He walked away and a minute later I saw Ms. Hamilton, the administrator in charge of the clinical trial, coming down the hall.

"Good morning, Mr. Roberts. Tom told me you are here for your second transplant appointment. According to your file, you received a Generator treatment yesterday morning. That violates one of the conditions of your control group, and I'm afraid you won't be able allowed to continue in the trial. I'm terribly sorry," she said.

I was shocked. "No, no. That's a mistake. I didn't really receive a Generator treatment. It was all . . ." I stopped myself realizing that I wasn't sure what I should say next. I knew I couldn't divulge what really happened. "Look, there's an explanation behind this. I need you to speak to my doctor; he'll clear it all up."

"Are you saying your NHD record is not correct? It plainly shows that you had a session yesterday," Ms. Hamilton said.

I was in the process of calling Dr. Steele's office, and I answered her a bit brusquely. "Yes, it's a mistake. Just give me a minute."

Dr. Steele's receptionist answered, "Dr. Steele's office. Can I help you?"

"Hello, this is Dave Roberts. Could I speak to Dr. Steele, please?"

"I'm sorry. He's with a patient. Can he call you back?"

"This is a bit of an emergency. Please tell him it concerns my stem cell transplant scheduled for this morning," I pleaded.

"Alright. Please hold."

A minute later Dr. Steele answered, "What's up, Dave? Are you okay?"

I explained the situation and he responded, "Oh, no! What was I thinking? Guardian Security informed me of their operation and that they had scheduled a phony appointment for you. I was supposed to go into the NHD and correct your record yesterday afternoon. I'm sorry, but I forgot to take care of it. Let me speak to the administrator."

Ms. Hamilton listened to Dr. Steele and then responded, "I'm sorry doctor. It's not that I don't believe you, but I need to see proper documentation before I can remove this 'hold' on Mr. Robert's record. If you can have Guardian Security send it to me in the next 15 minutes, we'll be able to proceed with today's appointment. Otherwise it will have to be rescheduled." There was a pause and then she handed me my MiNDi. "He wants to speak to you," she said.

"Yes, doctor. Can you make this work?" I said anxiously.

"I'm calling Guardian Security. We'll know in a minute," he said. I heard him speaking to someone, and then he said to me, "Dave, they're going to try and get a document sent to the hospital in the next ten minutes or so. Hang tight and wait for it. I've got to get back to my patient. Please call and let me know what happens. I'm really sorry about this. Forgive me."

To be honest, I was a little angry and didn't feel like being gracious. But I knew I had to forgive him. "It's okay, Dr. Steele. It was just an oversight. I'll call you later," I said and hung up. Then I said to Ms. Hamilton, "My doctor spoke to Guardian Security, and they will try and send a document to you within ten minutes."

"Okay, I'll wait," she said.

As I stood there waiting I asked God to help me. "Please make sure the document gets here in time," I asked him. Then I thought about how I had just reacted. Dr. Steele made a simple mistake and I got frustrated with him. As a result of his error, I might have to reschedule my appointment. That was pretty inconvenient. As I thought about it further, I realized how often I got angry when things didn't go as smoothly as I thought they should—especially when I thought someone else was to blame. In the past when I got frustrated and angry it never bothered me very much. But this time it was different. "Maybe God is trying to teach me another lesson," I thought. I made a mental note to look up anger in the Bible and see what God had to say about it.

The administrator was sitting quietly in front of the computer. After ten minutes she hadn't received the document. She waited five more minutes and then came over to me. "I'm sorry, Mr. Roberts, but it appears we'll have to reschedule your appointment. We can fit you in next Tuesday morning if that's convenient for you."

I felt myself getting angry again and let out a sigh of frustration. "Sure. I suppose that will have to do. Go ahead and put me down for Tuesday morning."

She glanced at me and said somewhat meekly, "I'm sorry; I hope you understand. I have to follow protocol."

I looked at her and realized that my response must have communicated that I was frustrated with her. I smiled and said, "Yes, of course I understand. It's not your fault. And thanks for taking time to try and help me."

Her face brightened and after a moment she said, "Look, I trust that your doctor will make sure the document is sent to me. I'm going to override this 'hold' on your record. Let me call the nurse to bring you to the exam room."

I couldn't believe it! I didn't expect her to take that kind of risk to help me. "But couldn't you get into trouble?" I asked.

"The document should arrive soon. I'm sure everything will be okay," she said.

All I could say was, "Thank you so much! I really appreciate it."

"You're welcome. The nurse will be here in a couple of minutes. I hope everything goes well."

I smiled and said, "Thanks again." Then I took a seat and told God how thankful I was. He had answered my prayer, but not the way I expected him to.

When the transfusion was done I had to wait 30 minutes in a recovery area before I could leave. Other than a tender spot where they injected me, I felt fine. As soon as I left the recovery area I turned on my MiNDi and saw that Kharis had called and left a message: "Breakthrough! Call me." I had about 15 minutes to get to the Imaging department for my 11:30 appointment, so I called Kharis while I was navigating the hospital's halls.

"Hello, Dave."

"Hello, Kharis. So tell me what's happened."

"There's good news. Guardian Security questioned one of Future Health's employees, a woman named Madelyn who works in the security department. They must have a good case against her because she called for a lawyer immediately. The last I heard they're trying to iron out a plea bargain with Guardian Justice. I'm on my way downtown to find out more. Do you want to come?"

"I'm at the hospital and I won't be free until 12:30 or so. I can come after that. Does Guardian Security think she's the person they're looking for?"

"They said that she is just a pawn. She is working with, or for, someone else. Apparently her role was to provide the Generator access codes. She may have also sabotaged the computer in the accounting department."

"How did Guardian figure out she was involved?" I asked.

"Proxy told me she was toward the top of a suspect list created by Guardian's computer. There were several threads that lead them to her. One of the strongest indicators was that she had access to the Generator codes. I don't have any more details, but Proxy thinks it's almost over. He says that she'll tell Guardian whatever they want to know, otherwise she'll spend the next 20 or 30 years in prison."

"It's too good to be true. I hope this really is the end. I'll be there when I'm done at the hospital. See you soon."

"Okay, Dave. See you."

The MRI took about 45 minutes. The technician told me that the radiologist would send the results to my doctor by 4:00 this afternoon. I hurried and got dressed, and then headed for my car.

When I arrived at Guardian Security's headquarters, Kharis came to the front desk to meet me. "Glad to see you, Dave. How did everything go at the hospital?" he asked.

"Fine. No problems. Anything new to report?"

"Plenty. The woman, Madelyn, agreed to a plea bargain with Guardian Justice. An agent reported part of her statement to us. She lost her son to malignancy about four years ago. A few months after her son's death, a man approached her, Dimitri is his name. He was working at Future Health as a computer consultant at that time. He told her that he occasionally worked as a consultant for a group of researchers who were trying to find a Generator formula to cure malignancy. The two of them met several times, and soon their relationship developed into something more intimate. Eventually Dimitri told her that this research group had discovered a formula that showed great promise for curing malignancy. They were wading through the bureaucratic process with the Ministry of Health so that they could begin testing their formula with the Generator. But Dimitri told her that the Ministry of Health was making it extremely difficult for researchers not associated with Future Health to get their Generator formulas tested and approved. He said that Future Health was using their money and influence in Washington to gain an unfair advantage."

"That sounds believable enough. Future Health must have plenty of politicians and lobby groups working on their behalf. How can anyone else compete with them?"

"Unfortunately, that's the way the game works. And that's why Madelyn empathized with the research group's predicament. She was outraged that the government was impeding progress in finding a cure for malignancy. Dimitri wanted her to help the group secretly gain access to the Generator so they could test their formula. She claimed that he showed her several documents to convince her that the formula was effective and safe in laboratory tests. She also asserted that neither Dimitri, nor anyone else offered to pay her, and that she wasn't interested in profiting from this in any way. She simply wanted to see a cure for malignancy."

At that point we entered into a dark room that had several large monitors on the walls, and I saw at least three agents busily at work. Proxy was sitting at a computer and when he saw us walk in, he came over.

"Welcome to the Operation's Room, Dave. How did it go at the hospital?"

"It went well; thanks for asking. You look beat. How long have you been here?"

"All night. I got a couple hours sleep on a sofa somewhere. Did Kharis fill you in?" Proxy asked.

"I was telling him about Madelyn's statement, but I didn't get to finish," Kharis responded.

"It will have to wait. We've got Guardian Security's D.C. bureau on that monitor," he said pointing to a large monitor in the center of the room. "Atlanta is on that monitor," he said pointing to another monitor. "And the NBA playoffs were on that monitor until an agent made me turn it off." I couldn't tell if he was joking or not. "They just started crunching this Dimitri guy and I want to find out what they've learned."

As we walked over to the central monitor I asked, "What does 'crunching' mean?"

Kharis answered, "They pull together all the electronic information they have on him, both current and historical, and run it through their computers to prepare a profile of him. It's like assembling a huge jigsaw puzzle of this guy's life."

When we were close to the monitor, we could hear the conversation between the agent in the room and the one in D.C.

"Jack, I'm guessing he's cleared passport control already. But you know how difficult it is to work with the FSB—especially after that fiasco in Prague last year. They won't let us connect to their security network. We'll have to wait to hear from them."

"How much longer, Ryan?" Jack asked.

"I don't know. But don't wander away. Who's that new guy standing by Max?"

Jack turned and saw me with Kharis and Proxy. He walked over to me and asked, "Who are you?"

Before I could answer, Proxy looked up at the central monitor and said loudly enough for Ryan to hear, "This is Dave. He's a friend of mine. Don't worry; he has clearance to be here. So what's this talk about passport control?"

Jack shook my hand and said, "Good to meet you, Dave. I'm Jack. Let's all sit down at the table." We sat down and Jack continued, "Dimitri boarded a plane in New York last night bound for Moscow. The plane landed over an hour ago. We contacted the FSB, that's Russia's security agency, and they notified passport control. We're waiting to hear if Dimitri has made it out of the airport yet. We've also alerted our agents in Moscow. But Russia is still a dark zone and if he's using a Russian MiNDi, I'm afraid we're going to be flying blind."

"What's a 'dark zone' and what do you mean you'll be flying blind?" I asked.

Most of our electronic tracking and surveillance operations are worthless in Russia. They won't allow us to use them, and they are extremely reluctant to share their data with us. The FSB keeps some electronic records, but the amount of data is limited, partly because they don't use Bio-chips in Russia. And we're flying blind because Dimitri left his MiNDi in his New York apartment. He's probably using a Russian model in Moscow. That means no GPS chip, and no ability to trace his calls—unless the FSB wants to share that information with us."

"That's just great. Any chance he'll escape?" Proxy asked.

The agent responded, "Not likely. But I'm sure he's been planning his getaway for some time. He knew he would eventually be discovered. It appears this ruse has been going on for quite some time." He paused and then said, "It's humiliating that we didn't detect it."

Proxy spoke, "We've been trying for years to warn the government that something was wrong with the Generator. How many lives could have been spared if someone had listened to us?"

Jack looked at him, but didn't say anything. Then another agent called out, "He made it through passport control. He's on the loose in Moscow."

Jack stood up, went to over to the monitor, and spoke to the agent in D.C. "Did you get that, Ryan?"

"Yes. We've got our agents on alert," Ryan responded.

Jack sat down in front of a computer and entered some keystrokes. "We still don't have access to Dimitri's employment file. Tom, contact the consulting firm again and tell them we need access to that file now! Let's see what we have on his connection to Moscow. He made thirteen trips there in the last five years. He stays ranged from 12 to 28 days. It looks like he made over a hundred phone calls to Russia in the last couple of years to family members, Life Force Technologies, and some unidentified numbers and Net addresses. Ryan, what did the FSB say about sending us more information?"

"We haven't heard from them yet. We've already sent them a partial workup on Dimitri. Let's hope they'll reciprocate," Ryan said.

"See what we can come up with on his family. It looks like several of the calls went to one of his sisters, Tanya, who lives in St. Petersburg."

Things quieted down for a few minutes so I asked Proxy what he knew about Dimitri.

"Only what I've been able to overhear. He's 38 years old. He immigrated to the U.S. 12 years ago. He lives alone in a Manhattan apartment, has never been married, and doesn't have children. He has two sisters and a brother, all of them still living in Russia, and some nieces and nephews. His parents are deceased. He works for an international computer consulting firm. He has worked as a consultant at Future Health off and on over the last seven years in the accounting department. He's also worked at several other companies here in the States and overseas. He specializes in international finance and accounting applications. For the last few years he's been spending a lot of time with Madelyn. Sometimes she visited him in New York, and sometimes he visited her in Atlanta. That's the important information I picked up," Proxy said.

Just then I saw Ryan on the large monitor again. "Hey, Jack. Look what the computer just spit out. Just over four years ago a Russian based medical device company applied to the Ministry of Health requesting permission to market their frequency generator here in the U.S. Their request was denied. What do you think? Should I inform the FSB?"

"Is there some connection between this company and Dimitri?" Jack asked.

"He's worked as a consultant for them for the last six years," the agent responded.

"Go ahead and call them. Ask them to send us all the information they have on that company. What's the name of it?" Jack asked.

"Life Force Technologies," Ryan responded.

Jack turned back to his computer and a few minutes later motioned for us to come over. We walked up to him and he said, "Look at this." There were several items on the monitor. The first one said, "Life Force Technologies has signed an exclusive contract with the Health Ministry of Japan to provide its Force III Generator to national hospitals and clinics." The next one said, "China has announced plans to purchase hundreds of frequency generators over the next several years. Future Health, Life Force Technologies of Russia, and Precision Medical of Germany are all competing for the exclusive government contract."

There were more entries, but Jack said, "Do you see what's happening? Currently there are only three companies in the world producing frequency generators. Can you imagine what it would be worth to sign a contract with China to sell hundreds of them? It must be a multi-million dollar market."

Proxy spoke, "And somebody is taking extreme measures to gain a competitive edge. Future Health just suffered a major blow and might be out of contention."

"Right," Jack said. "I need to talk to Ryan about this. We need to be careful. If Life Force Technologies is responsible for sabotaging Future Health's generator and showing utter disregard for the well-being of thousands of people, then there's no telling what they are capable of."

Jack went to talk to Ryan privately and we stayed at the table. I hadn't eaten any lunch and was feeling a little weak. "Is there a place to get some juice around here?" I asked.

"I saw some vending machines somewhere. Let's take a walk," Kharis replied. Proxy went back to the computer he was at earlier, and Kharis and I went to find the vending machine. We found a small lunchroom and sat down to have a snack. I called Monika and tried to summarize what had happened. She was astounded.

"Guardian Security's Operation's Room, the FSB, corporate sabotage . . . what's next? This is incredible!" she said.

"Maybe I'll write a book," I said jokingly.

"So how are you holding up?" she asked.

"I'm feeling a little tired, but it's pretty exciting around here. The adrenaline is keeping me going."

"When will you hear the results of your MRI?" she asked.

"The technician said Dr. Steele would have the results by 4:00. I'll probably stay here until then."

"Okay, but don't overdo it. And call me when you can. I'm just sitting at my desk, so you won't be interrupting anything."

"Alright. I'll call when I know more. Bye."

Kharis and I finished our snack and headed back to the Operation's Room. As we walked in there was a lot of commotion. Ryan was on the central monitor speaking to Jack. We heard him say, "The police said he was alone in his hotel room. They claim it was a robbery. They took his money, and no computer or MiNDi was found in the room. That's all we have right now. It's almost midnight there, so I'm going to wait until the morning to send someone to talk to them."

Jack appeared agitated. He said to Ryan, "This was no robbery. It had to be a professional hit. Have you mobilized?"

Ryan responded, "I ordered direct surveillance on Dimitri's family members. All ops are now covert, and we've cut off the flow of information to the FSB."

"I want hourly reports," Jack responded.

Proxy was standing near Jack, and as Kharis and I walked toward them, he saw us and came over. "We just found out that Dimitri was killed," he said quietly.

"Killed!" I said.

Kharis asked, "Do they have any idea who did it?"

"No. But Jack said it appears to be an execution," Proxy replied.

"So does that mean it's all over?" I asked.

Jack walked over and said, "Gentlemen, I was afraid of this. There was too much at stake. They couldn't let a principal player like Dimitri get caught. He knew too much."

"Who are 'they'?" I asked.

"We have to assume it's Life Force Technologies, or someone associated with them. It's going to be difficult to prove that though without Dimitri. Maybe we'll turn up some evidence as we continue investigating, or possibly the FSB will cooperate and share what they have on him. But I wouldn't count on the latter."

I felt deflated, like all my emotional energy had drained out of me. Proxy and Kharis both looked discouraged and tired.

"I think I'm going to head home. Can someone contact me if anything important happens?" I asked.

Proxy answered, "Jack, will you keep in touch with me? I'll contact Dave and Kharis. I'm ready to get some rest myself."

"Of course. I'll have someone contact you. We should know more by the morning, after one of our agents meets with the police. Sorry, but this doesn't look like it will end well," Jack said.

Proxy, Kharis, and I walked out together. Kharis offered to drive Proxy to his hotel, so I said goodbye and walked to my car. As I drove home, I called Monika and told her what happened.

"What a shame. It appears that he was guilty of heinous crimes, but to die like that! How awful," Monika said.

"I'm not sure I share your sentiments. Now that he's dead, I'm worried that the real criminals might never be caught."

"Won't the Russian police investigate?" she asked.

"I suppose so. It doesn't sound very hopeful though. I'm tired. I'm going to go home and rest. What time do you think you'll get home?"

"The usual time, 6:15 or so. Do you feel like eating supper?"

"I don't right now, but I think I will by dinner time."

"Why don't I pick up some take-out on the way home?"

"Thanks, that would be fine. I'll see you soon. Bye, honey."

"Bye, Davey."

I got home around 3:30. I stretched out on the couch to rest for a half hour before calling Dr. Steele to find out about my MRI results. I woke up two hours later. I quickly called the clinic, but Dr. Steele had already left. I had his emergency number, but decided not to call it. I sent him a message instead. I felt hungry, so I grabbed a banana and went out on the patio to wait for Monika.

The day's events ran through my mind, and I imagined how some of the pieces of the puzzle might fit together. Dimitri had worked as a consultant for Life Force Technologies and for Future Health for several years, so it was easy to see how he might have been recruited by the Russian company to sabotage the Generator. While he was at Future Health he singled out Madelyn as someone who could help him gain access to the Generator codes. Maybe he saw that she was especially vulnerable after the death of her son. He managed to win her affections, and then he manipulated her into providing him with the Generator codes or the means to steal them. He was responsible for getting the codes to Life Force Technologies, and then they sabotaged the Generator. Maybe they were testing experimental formulas on other people, but they deliberately used a formula on me that was known to damage healthy cells. I wondered if Dimitri ever knew that formulas were being secretly sent to the Generator and that some of them were actually harming people. Just then Monika came home.

I stepped into the house to greet her. "Hi, honey. You're early."

"I was anxious to get home, so I splurged on a taxi. Why didn't you call me? What did Dr. Steele say?"

"Sorry for not calling. I fell asleep, and by the time I called the clinic, he had left. I sent him a message to call me as soon as possible."

"You must have been exhausted. How are you feeling now?"

"Well rested. I'll probably be up until midnight. Let's eat, I'm hungry."

Monika and I sat down to dinner and discussed the day's events while we ate. "So Guardian Security believes Dimitri was working for Life Force Technologies, and that they are responsible for his death?" Monika asked.

"That's what Jack, one of the special agents, said. He thought Dimitri knew too much and had to be silenced. It makes sense. I wonder if we'll ever find out what was really going on now that he's dead," I said.

"And I wonder if anyone will ever be punished for all these atrocities."

"The only bright side is that the Ministry of Health must be questioning the safety of the Generator. That's what this was all about, remember? Getting them to open an investigation."

Just then Hailey announced, "Dr. Steele is calling. Connect?"

"Connect!" I practically shouted.

I walked over to the kitchen monitor and said, "Hello, Dr. Steele."

"Good evening, Dave. I'm sure you're anxious to hear the results of the MRI. I'm sorry, but the radiologist did not send me the results this afternoon. I called the hospital around 5:00 and was told the results won't be available until tomorrow morning. It's disappointing, I know. I'll call you tomorrow as soon as I get the report."

"Okay. I guess I can wait one more day. I'll talk to you in the morning. Thanks for calling."

"You're welcome. And sorry again for the mix-up at the hospital. How are you feeling?"

"I'm feeling okay. I was just tired this afternoon."

"Try and get enough rest. Do you still have some sleeping pills?"

"Yes, I've got some left."

"Okay, good. Then I'll call you tomorrow morning."

A few minutes later Jasmine called. She was anxious to hear the results of my scan and was disappointed to hear that I didn't have them yet. I spent almost an hour talking to her and explaining everything that happened. She took the news calmly.

"Murder is pretty extreme, but it doesn't shock me. Some of these corporations act as if they are above the law. They have no conscience. Profits are all that concern them," she said.

"I'm sure there's some truth to what you're saying. But I think those corporations are the exception, not the rule," I said.

"Maybe, maybe not. Anyhow, I want to hear the results of your scan as soon as you find out what they are. Do you promise to call me right away?"

"As soon as I can. I'm sure it will be sometime tomorrow morning."

"I'll be waiting. Love you, Dad. Bye."

"I love you, too, Jaz. Goodbye."

After talking to Jasmine, Monika and I went for a long walk. Either the fresh air and exercise tired me out, or I was worn out from all the day's excitement because I didn't have any trouble getting to sleep that night.

Chapter 30

Conclusion

Monika was still asleep when I got out of bed at 6:15. I went into the kitchen and started brewing some coffee, then checked for messages. Kharis had left a message at 4:37 that morning saying, "Call me. I'm in the Operation's Room." I quickly called him.

"Hello, Kharis. What's going on?"

"Dave, Dimitri's sister and her husband were both gunned down a couple of hours ago. They were trying to leave the country and were killed when they arrived at the train station. A Guardian Security agent had them under observation and witnessed the shootings."

"What! Why were they killed? What is going on?" I said in astonishment.

"I can't discuss that over the Net. Can you come here?" Kharis asked.

"Yes, I can come. I'll leave in a few minutes."

"Okay. See you soon."

I went to the bedroom to get dressed and Monika was awake. "What happened? I heard you talking to someone."

I gave her the news and she looked like she was in a state of shock. "What in heaven's name is going on? This can't be real."

"I'm going downtown to see what they can tell me. I'll call you as soon as I can."

"What about work? Don't you have an important meeting today?"

"That's not until this afternoon. I'll be there for it."

I dashed out and made it downtown in 20 minutes. I walked into the Operation's Room and saw Kharis and Proxy talking to Jack. As I joined them Jack said, "Dave, what I'm going to tell you can't be shared with anyone else. You must agree to remain silent. Do you understand?"

"Can I tell my wife?"

"Yes, but nobody else."

"What's going on?" I asked.

"You heard about Dimitri's sister and her husband. They had just purchased train tickets to Helsinki and gotten a taxi to the train station. One of our agents had them under surveillance. They arrived at the train station and were getting out of the taxi when a black Mercedes pulled up behind them. A man got out and started to approach them. They jumped back in to the taxi. The man tried to open the door, but it was locked. He pulled a gun, shot threw the window, and killed them both. Then he ran back to the car and sped off."

I shook my head in disbelief. "Why were they killed? And why is that information so sensitive?" I asked.

"Let's sit down," Jack said. We sat at the table and Jack continued. "After you left yesterday I did some further checking into Life Force Technologies. I should have done it sooner, but I doubt it would have changed anything. The business is owned by Yuri Ivanov. His brother-in-law is Alexander Fedorov. Does that name sound familiar?"

"I think I've heard it on the news, but I don't remember who he is," I answered.

"He's the leader of a major political party and is running for president. He's also a former FSB associate director. He left the agency a couple of years ago."

I stared at Jack and thought about what he said. "I can see where you're going. You think the FSB is behind these killings, right?" I asked.

"We know they are. This morning we intercepted a message that was sent to Madelyn from Tanya, that's Dimitri's sister who was executed. Dimitri sent a document to her shortly after he arrived in Moscow, and she sent it to Madelyn just before leaving for the train station. It was encrypted, but Madelyn had the key."

"What was in the document?" I asked.

Jack answered, "The first part was a personal message to Madelyn. I won't share that with you, but he apologized for deceiving her and involving her in all of this. He also admitted that he fell in love with her. The second part of the message was meant for us. He explained how he was recruited by the FSB. They approached him when he was working as a computer consultant at Life Force Technologies and asked him to serve his country by working as a corporate spy. They knew he had signed a multi-year contract to work as a computer consultant at Future Health, which is why they chose him. The objective was to steal information from Future Health's research and development department. He confessed that he was offered a large sum of money, which made it easier to say 'yes' to their request. His assignments were to install some programs on computers in Future Health's headquarters and to figure out how to connect to the computers in the R&D department. According to him, that part was relatively easy. Then the FSB gave him another assignment: obtain the access codes to the Generator. That's when he became suspicious and wanted to quit."

Kharis said sarcastically, "I'm sure the FSB was happy to accept his resignation."

Jack replied, "You don't say 'no' to the FSB. But he tried. He told them he didn't think he had the computer expertise to steal the codes. They threatened him, telling him that all the money he had placed in a Russian bank would be confiscated, and that their operatives in the U.S would make his life very uncomfortable. He reluctantly agreed to try, but he wasn't able to get at the codes. At that point the FSB told him to find another way. They said his brother and sisters, and their children, would pay a price if he failed. He was terrified and didn't know what to do. He told them he'd try again."

"Is that where Madelyn came into the picture," I asked.

Jack replied, "That's right, but he doesn't go into much detail about it. Maybe he felt guilty for using her. When he succeeded in obtaining the codes, the FSB was very pleased. They told him that he was a good patriot, and that he was helping to find a cure for malignancy. But he knew that providing them with the Generator codes had nothing to do with finding a cure for malignancy, and that they had ulterior motives. He had discovered that Life Force

Technologies was owned by Ivanov, and figured that he and his brother-in-law, Fedorov, must be plotting something together. Fedorov was likely issuing orders to the FSB, or at least some of his comrades who still worked there, and somehow he planned to profit from this scheme—either financially or politically, or maybe both."

"But he kept providing them with the codes," Kharis said.

"The codes were changed every 90 days, and the FSB needed him to continue his deception with Madelyn. He didn't have much choice. The threats to his family were very real."

"Did he ever realize that the formulas being sent by the FSB were harming people?" I asked. "Apparently not. He believed that the FSB was trying to undermine Future Health's success by sabotaging the Generator. But based on what he wrote, he assumed that they were simply causing the Generator to malfunction. There's no indication that he ever suspected they were intentionally sending formulas known to cause cell damage," Jack answered.

"The fact that he believed they were causing the Generator to malfunction should have been enough to trigger a response. He should have warned someone about it. As a result of his actions, he knew that people were not receiving the treatment they needed. He got what he deserved," Proxy said with disgust.

"Yes, he probably did," Jack said.

"And what happens now? Is there any hope that Ivanov or Fedorov will ever be convicted?"

"I sincerely doubt it. But that's out of our hands. We sent Dimitri's document along with a preliminary report to the administration this morning. We'll have to wait and see what happens next."

"Do you mean to Guardian Security's administrators?" I asked.

"I meant to the president. This is a matter for the State Department and the Committee on Foreign Relations to handle," Jack answered.

"They'll issue a statement condemning their actions. Maybe give them a slap on the wrist. Nothing more," Proxy said.

"What about the press? Will they be informed?" Kharis asked.

Jack quickly glanced at Proxy and then looked at Kharis, "That's not my decision to make. But the public needs to know the whole story. Gentlemen, I have to report to my boss in a few minutes. If you have any questions, they'll have to wait. I know it isn't much, but you'll receive commendations from our department for your efforts in uncovering this plot. I strongly recommend that you stick them in a drawer somewhere, and that you try and maintain some degree of anonymity in regards to this case—at least for the time being. Do you understand?"

We looked at each other, and then nodded in agreement.

"Don't worry, it will blow over in a few months," Jack said as he stood up. We all shook hands and then Jack started to leave.

Before he walked away I asked him, "Do you think there's any chance these guys will be prosecuted?"

"I'll give you my honest opinion. There will be a feeble attempt at investigating the murders, but no one will be charged. We have one incriminating document and a dead witness. Unless we can come up with some solid evidence, the case would never stand up in the International Court of Justice. And even if it did, Russia isn't likely to abide by its ruling," Jack replied. "And besides, Fedorov is one of the strongest pro-democracy candidates in the pack and has plenty of supporters in Washington. You can probably figure out the rest."

"I expected as much. I think I need a cup of coffee," I said.

Proxy stood up and said, "You two go ahead. I've got some important business to take care of. I'll talk to you both soon." Then he left.

Kharis and I watched him walk away, and then we headed toward the lunchroom. "Not the most sociable guy, but I still like him," Kharis said.

"He kind of grows on you after a while," I responded.

Kharis and I grabbed a cup of coffee and talked as we walked toward the exit. When we were out on the street he said, "I promised to give Maria an update as soon as I could. I'm going to stop by her office. Are you going to work?"

"Yes, I've got some things to take care of today. And I'm supposed to hear from my doctor this morning about the results of yesterdays scan."

"Will you call me and let me know what he says?"

"Sure." I gave him a strong handshake and said, "Now that this is over, I hope our friendship will continue."

"It's just starting. What about you and Monika coming to church with me this Sunday?"

"Maybe we will. I'll let you know later."

"Great. I'll talk to you soon. See you, Dave."

"See you, Kharis."

As I drove to work I called Monika and told her what happened. She listened calmly and didn't say anything. When I finished I said, "You're awfully quiet."

"As soon as you told me about Fedorov and the FSB I could have guessed the outcome. It's the same old story. I stopped being shocked by such abuses of power a long time ago. Just think of all the lives that were affected. And nothing will be done about it," she said.

"Probably not, although I wouldn't rule out a lawsuit against Future Health. But financial restitution doesn't begin to make up for the loss of life and suffering that took place."

"No, it doesn't. And with Future Health under scrutiny and all the bad publicity aimed at them, that Russian medical company will probably rake in huge profits, and the bad guys will end up laughing all the way to the bank."

"It does looks like their plan worked," I said.

"I could stand some good news. I don't suppose Dr. Steele has called yet?"

"No, I don't expect I'll hear from him until late morning. I'll call you as soon as I know anything."

"I'll be waiting. Love you."

"Love you, too."

I got to work and stopped by Julia's office. She smiled when she saw me and asked me to come in. "Good morning, Dave. Are you okay? You look tired."

"Do you have a few minutes?" I asked.

"Sure. Sit down. What's on your mind?"

As I told her the story, she seemed incredulous. At one point she said angrily, "Are you're telling me that their actions are responsible for infecting everyone with malignancy?"

"No, we don't know that for sure. It's possible they were sending experimental formulas to the Generator searching for a cure for malignancy, although the formula that was used on me was clearly harmful. But at this point nobody knows how many treatments were sabotaged, or what affect the formulas they used might have had. And we might never know."

"But what about the rise in the number of malignancy cases in recent years? It has to be their fault, doesn't it?"

"It may be to some degree. But even if someone could determine which formulas were used, I think it would be difficult to prove that they caused malignancy. And the fact is the sabotage operation began less than three years ago. Malignancy started appearing over five years ago."

Julia nodded, "That's true. So the cause is still a mystery."

"I'm afraid so. But there does seem to be a clear connection between Generator exposure and malignancy. It needs to be investigated."

"Isn't Future Health doing that?" she asked.

"Supposedly. But the public is demanding an official investigation by the Ministry of Health. Even with all of Future Health's resources and influence in Washington, I don't see how they can avoid it. In any case, I hope they'll be able to find the problem and get it fixed quickly."

She nodded in agreement. "So do I. The Generator has helped so many people. I personally know three women who had their cancer cured by it, and a coworker who was healed of hepatitis. We all accept that there are risks involved with other medical procedures like surgery, or even taking medications. Maybe the risks of Generator exposure are worth the benefits."

"I hadn't looked at it from that perspective, and you might be right. I think the public just wants to have a better idea of what the risks are. Doctors should provide us with the data and let us make an informed choice."

"Exactly. After all, doctors are only practicing medicine. There are no guarantees. And speaking of doctors, have you heard from your doctor yet?"

"He's supposed to call this morning. I'll let you know what he says."

"Please let me know when you hear from him. So, are you ready for the meeting this afternoon?"

"I think so. I just need to review my presentation and make sure it's ready." As I stood up to leave I asked, "You'll be there, won't you?"

"Yes. I've got it on my schedule."

"I'll see you at 2:00 then. And thanks for listening, Julia. Will you keep this to yourself for now? I wasn't supposed to share it with anyone yet."

"I won't say a word. Nobody would believe me anyhow."

I grinned and said, "No, I don't expect that they would."

I walked to my office and saw I had a message to call Laura in HR. I decided to wait to call her and started working on my presentation. Dr. Steele called a half hour later. I took a deep breath before answering. "Good morning, Dr. Steele."

"Good morning, Dave. Are you ready for this?" he asked.

His tone of voice seemed uncharacteristically lighthearted, and instantly my hopes soared. I think my heart must have skipped a beat as I responded, "Yes, I'm ready."

"You've been designated M-125. There's been a marked reduction of malignant cells. Your pancreas responded to the stem cell transplant at an above normal rate, and it will likely continue to do so. It looks like you'll be another one of their success stories in a few weeks."

I wanted to jump up and shout, but had second thoughts when I saw my office door was open. "Are you sure about that?" I asked.

"The M-125 diagnosis is conservative. An MRI doesn't provide quite the same level of detail as a Generator scan, so the computer has a larger margin of error and takes that into account when calculating a diagnosis. You could very well be M-150," Dr. Steele explained.

"That's incredible! I wish Monika and my kids were here. I've got to call them right away. Is there anything else you need to tell me?"

"Just that you need to schedule an appointment with me soon. Early next week if possible. We need to run some routine tests. You don't need to concern yourself with it right now; go ahead and celebrate."

"I will. Thanks so much, doctor. I'll see you next week," I said.

I quickly placed a conference call to Monika, Jasmine, and Lori. Monika came on first, "Hello, Dave. Is this the call I've been waiting for?"

"Yes, just wait one more minute. I'm calling Jasmine and Lori as well," I said.

"Can't you give me a hint? Thumbs up or down, or something?" Monika asked.

Just then Jasmine joined the call, and a few seconds I saw Lori's face on my monitor.

"Hi, Dad and Mom," Lori said.

"Dad, did you hear anything?" Jasmine asked.

"How does M-125 sound?" I said.

"Yes!!" Jasmine shouted.

"Way to go, Dad," Lori said.

"Davey, that's wonderful! I'm so happy for you," Monika said.

"Isn't it amazing? And Dr. Steele was very positive. He said that my response was above average, and that it would most likely continue. The news couldn't be any better."

"You've got your life back! Why don't you take the rest of the day off and we'll celebrate?" Monika suggested.

"I've got an important meeting at 2:00. I'm announcing to my department that I will be terminated in four weeks. I gave my M-60 notice, remember?" I said.

"Isn't there some way to rescind that? You only notified them a couple of days ago?" Monika asked.

"No. It's been entered into my personnel file. But I'm too happy to let that spoil my day. The meeting will be finished by 4:00. I'll leave right after it's over and pick you up. Let's plan on going out to dinner. Lori can you join us?"

"I wish I could, but I have to work. How about I bring dessert over to your house around 7:00," Lori said.

"That would be great. And bring Caleb if he wants to join us," I said.

"I will," Lori responded.

"Jasmine, we'll miss you, but I'll talk to you this weekend. I want to start planning a trip to Colorado," I said.

"Just name the date and I'll make all the arrangements," she said.

"I have to wait until the stem cell trial is over. I'll think about it. I better say goodbye for now. I love you all," I said.

"Bye, Dad. I love you," Jasmine said.

"See you tonight, Dad. Love you," Lori said.

"Give me a call when you leave work. I'll see you around 4:30. Love you, Davey," Monika said.

I called Owen next and gave him the news. "Way to go, bro! I knew you could do it. So does this mean you're out of the woods?" he asked.

"I've got three weeks of stem cell therapy left, but my doctor was really encouraging. He thinks I'll be alright."

"I'm glad to know you're going to be around for a long time. So how about lunch again soon?

"I'd like that. Maybe next weekend. I'll give you a call."

"Okay. And don't forget, it's your turn to buy."

"It'll be my pleasure. I'll talk to you later."

I wanted to call Kharis, but all of a sudden I was really hungry and decided to wait until after lunch. I walked by Julia's office, but she wasn't there. I went downstairs to the cafeteria and had an early lunch. After lunch I walked by the HR office and stopped in to see if Laura was there. She was at her desk.

"Hi, Laura. How are you?" I asked.

"Hi, Dave. I'm doing well. What about you?"

"I'm doing great. I got your message. What did you need to talk to me about?" I asked.

"I wanted to ask how your appointment went. It was yesterday, right?"

"Yes, it was. Thanks for asking," I said, and then I told her the good news.

She responded, "Dave, that's fantastic. I've heard so many good things about stem cell therapy, and I was hoping it would work for you. You must be ecstatic!"

"You could say that. And I'm not even worried about being unemployed in a few weeks—at least not today."

"You don't need to worry about that at all," she said and smiled. "After you notified me of your M-60 status a couple of days ago, I decided to hold off on updating your personnel file for a couple of days. I figured if this stem cell stuff worked, there was a good chance your 'M' status could change for the better. It looks like my gamble paid off."

I was astounded and humbled at the same time. I leaned over and said quietly, "Laura, why did you do it? You took a big risk."

"Not really. Technically I didn't break any rules. You were supposed to either update the file yourself, or notify HR in writing. You didn't do either; you just asked me to update your file—and I'm awfully absent-minded," she said with a laugh. "Besides, I planned to update your file after speaking to you today."

I smiled at her and said, "I always suspected you had a slightly rebellious streak in you. Maybe I'm prejudiced, but it's probably because of that tricked out Harley you drive."

"I think you are prejudiced. And I consider myself to be a non-conformist. Either way, aren't you glad?"

"I wish I knew how to thank you. I don't know what else could make this day any better. You're a gem."

"Glad to do it. And this is our little secret, okay?"

"I'll have to explain it to my boss somehow," I said.

"Your boss is Julia, right?"

"That's right."

"They don't come any more understanding than her. Go ahead and tell her what happened; she won't say a word to anyone."

"No, she won't. I'm going up to see her right now." I turned to leave and said, "Hey, how about a ride on that bike sometime?"

She looked pleased and said, "Anytime. I'll even let you drive it if you'd like to."

"You're on! I've always dreamed of taking a spin on a Harley."

I stopped by Julia's office again and she was just on her way out. "Hi, Julia. Are you on your way to lunch?" I asked.

"Hi, Dave. I was, but it can wait. Come in and have a seat. So, did you talk to your doctor?"

When I told her the good news she came up and gave me a hug. "Dave, you're going to be alright. Thank God. To be honest, I was scared you might die. I'm so happy for you."

"Thanks, Julia. I thought this might be my time, too, but I wasn't afraid. I know there is a much better life waiting for me."

She smiled. "You have a strong faith, Dave. I guess heaven will have to wait a little longer."

"I have more good news," I said and told her what Laura had done.

"Dave, you've made my day! And what a day you must be having. You need to celebrate. Why don't you take the afternoon off? You're going to cancel the meeting, aren't you?"

I thought about that for a second and then said, "No, I want to go ahead with the meeting and share what I've been going through with my team. They deserve to know I'm battling malignancy. But there's no reason for you to be there."

"But I'm part of your team, too. I'll be there," she said and stood up. "Do you want to join me downstairs for lunch?"

I got up and replied, "Thanks, but I just finished. I'll see you at 2:00."

"Okay, I'll see you soon," she said. And as I walked toward the door she added, "And welcome back, Dave."

I smiled and said, "It's great to be back."

When I got back to my office I called Kharis. "Hello, Dave," he said.

"Hi, Kharis. Am I interrupting anything?"

"Nothing that can't wait. So did you hear from your doctor?"

"Yes, I did," I said and gave him the good news.

"Dave, that's great news. So, it looks like God's plan for your life isn't finished yet. He has more for you to do."

"I suppose so, but I hope whatever lies ahead won't be quite as wild as this was."

Kharis laughed and said, "It was an adventure, to say the least. Dave, I'm meeting Maria and Proxy later today. Is it okay to update them or would you rather do it yourself?"

"Please fill them in for me. I've got a meeting to prepare for, so I'm a little pressed for time."

"Okay, then I'd better let you go. I'll talk to you soon."

"Thanks, Kharis. Bye."

I checked the time and saw that the meeting was less than two hours away. I needed to rethink my presentation. I wanted to take some time to share about my personal journey over the last few weeks, but I decided not to go into much detail. There was no need to share the whole story. I could use the extra time to discuss the plan I had been working on to restructure our customer service operations. I hadn't made much progress on it, but this would be a good opportunity to see what everyone else was thinking.

I was still hard at work at 2:00 and the presentation wasn't nearly ready. I went into the meeting feeling unprepared and surprisingly nervous about talking about my illness. Julia must have noticed something, because she came up to me and asked me how I was doing.

"A little nervous. Do you think I'm doing the right thing? Talking about my illness I mean. I'm wondering how everyone will react and what they'll think," I said.

"I think you made the right decision to tell them, and I think you'll be surprised by their reaction," Julia said. "But if you've changed your mind, that's okay, too."

I looked at people chatting around the table. I'd known many of them for quite a few years and considered several to be good friends. If one of them had malignancy I would want them to trust me and tell me about it. "You know what? I trust these people. Let's start the meeting, Julia," I said.

We started the meeting and I began by telling everyone about my M-100 diagnosis. There were a few quiet gasps, but by the time I finished and announced my reclassification to M-125 there were loud cheers and applause. It was very encouraging and I wondered what I had been nervous about. It took a few minutes to get the meeting back on course, but we ended up having a lively and beneficial discussion about how to approach the restructuring of our operations. Four o'clock rolled around before I knew it, and I dismissed the meeting. Several people stopped to talk to me on the way out and it was after 4:30 by the time I left to meet Monika.

Monika and I went out for a light supper and then went home to wait for Lori. She was late, as usual, and showed up around 7:30. We gathered in the kitchen and while Lori was preparing to serve dessert, I told them I had some more good news. I called Jasmine so I could share it with all three of them at the same time. Then I told them what Laura had done, and that my M-60 status had never been reported. They were elated and all started talking at once.

"So your job isn't in jeopardy! I was so worried about you," Monika said.

"Couldn't she have lost her job?" Lori asked.

"Dad, you have some good people working at your company," Jasmine said.

As we were talking, I was notified that Kharis was calling. "You three go on talking. I'm going to take this call in the office," I said. I walked into the office and answered his call. "Hello, Kharis."

"Hi, Dave. I wanted to let you know that I gave Proxy and Maria the update. Maria wanted to know if we could all get together for coffee Saturday morning. Are you and Monika busy?"

I checked with Monika and then replied, "We'd enjoy that. Where and when do you want to meet?"

"How does 8:00 sound at our typical spot, the Stone Hearth Coffeehouse?" Kharis asked.

"That sounds good. We'll be there," I answered.

"Great. See you in the morning."

I went back to the kitchen and Monika, Lori and Jasmine were still talking. Lori had served the pie and I could see that Jasmine had served herself some ice cream.

"You don't mind if I join you for dessert, do you?" Jasmine asked.

"I wouldn't mind a scoop of that ice cream on my pie," I quipped.

"They'll probably come up with a way to send that across the Net one of these days," she replied.

We all sat down to eat our dessert and spent a great evening together as a family.

Chapter 31
Epilogue

I woke up Saturday morning and got out of bed quietly in order not to disturb Monika. I hadn't slept so well in weeks and couldn't wait to get the day started. I made some coffee, picked up my Bible, and went outside on the porch to enjoy the cool morning.

As I sat there listening to the birds and feeling the breeze on my face, I could feel a sense of gratitude welling up inside. Words of praise and thanksgiving to God filled my thoughts, and his joy filled my heart. I wondered if I would have ever come to know him if I hadn't been infected with malignancy, or gotten involved with CAGE, or met Kharis. Why had God been so good to me? I wished I could do more to show him how thankful I was. Then I thought about Maria's husband and Julia's sister-in-law who both died of malignancy, and I wondered why they weren't cured, and more importantly, if they knew Jesus. Was there a 'Kharis' in their lives? I was pondering questions that were too profound for me, and I didn't know how to begin answering them. But one thing I did know: I wanted the rest of my life to be spent for something worthwhile. It didn't matter if God had big plans or small plans for me. What mattered was following him and honoring him in everything I did. And that seemed like the best way to express my gratitude for all that he had done for me. Just then I heard the door creak and Monika stepped out onto the porch.

"Good morning," I said.

"Good morning. It's going to be a beautiful day," she said.

"It sure is."

"What were you thinking about?" she asked.

I thought about how to answer her question for a moment and then said, "How inadequate words can be sometimes. And how meaningless our words can be if our actions aren't consistent with them."

"Wow! You're in a philosophical mood this morning. I'm afraid it's too early for me to enter in to a deep discussion. Plus I haven't had my coffee yet."

"That's okay. We can continue it later."

"That would be fun. Do you think we can set aside the whole day to spend together?"

"I was thinking the same thing. If the weather holds we could go for a hike or a bike ride this afternoon."

"And then our favorite ice cream shop?" she suggested.

"Good idea. But right now I'm feeling more like breakfast," I said and stood up. "I'm going to shower and get dressed. We need to leave soon."

"Okay, I'll be ready in 20 minutes," Monika said as we went inside together.

When we got to the coffeehouse Maria, Proxy, and Kharis were sitting at an outdoor table. We walked over and when Kharis saw us he said, "Good morning, Dave. And good morning, Monika. Have a seat."

Maria stood up and smiled at us. She came up to Monika kissed her on the cheek, and then did the same to me and gave me a quick hug. "Dave, it's wonderful news. I'm happy for you, and for Monika," she said.

Then Proxy came over and gave me one of his crushing handshakes. I grimaced, and as I introduced him to Monika I said, "I'd recommend kissing her hand, not shaking it." He let out a huge laugh and people on the street turned to stare at him. Then he gently took her hand and kissed it.

"Enchanté," he said.

Monika smiled and replied, "And I'm pleased to meet you."

"You've got yourself a good man here. We wouldn't be here celebrating our victory today without his help," Proxy said.

I was a little confused by what Proxy said. As we all sat down I asked, "What did you mean by that?"

"Maria heard yesterday evening that the Ministry of Health is launching a full scale investigation of the Generator. They plan to announce it publicly sometime today. We've finally accomplished our goal," Proxy explained.

"That's great! Congratulations. You've all worked a long time for this. So now that you've achieved your objective, what's next?" I asked.

"We'll be monitoring their investigation as much as possible. And we've already requested that all statistics related to Generator exposure, both historical and in the future, be made available to the public. There's still some resistance to that proposal, but we expect it will be implemented as long as patient privacy rights are respected. So we've still got some work to do," Maria answered.

"Does that mean CAGE is back in business?" Monika asked.

"No. We're not sure yet how the case will work out. But if we have to, it shouldn't be hard to start a new advocacy group and find plenty of support for our cause. Max is already looking into that," Maria responded.

"Do you ever take a day off?" I asked Proxy.

"I plan to spend the whole day with my wife tomorrow," he replied.

"So you're leaving?" I asked.

"I have a 3:30 flight. But I'll be back in a few weeks. Kharis wants to try his hand in the computer consulting field and I'm going to help him get started," Proxy answered.

"Then he's in good hands," I said.

"He's been in good hands for a few years now. I hope I can learn more from him than he can from me," Proxy said.

Kharis smiled at me and said, "Don't forget to pray for this guy. He's a tough nut to crack."

"You can count on it," I said. "So Kharis, will you continue to work with CAGE, I mean for the new group once it's formed?"

"I plan to help out in some capacity for the next few months. But I have a feeling that God has something new for me to do. I just don't know what it is yet," Kharis responded.

"So you don't plan on moving away anytime soon," Monika asked.

"No, not right now. I'll just have to wait and see what happens," Kharis replied.

As Monika and Kharis were talking I noticed a black sedan pull up and park in front of the coffeehouse. Two men got out, and one was holding some kind of device and looking toward us. They came over to us and we all looked at them.

"Is there a Maximus Rodriquez here?" one of them asked as he showed us his police badge.

"That would be me," Max said.

"Please come with us. You're wanted downtown for questioning," the man said.

Max looked at Maria, "Maria, my wife will kill me if I miss my plane. Get me out of this!"

Maria shook her head slowly, "Oh, Maximo. You better go with them. But don't worry; I'll have one of our lawyers meet you downtown. Then I'll call Guardian Security and see what they can do. Maybe you can still make your flight."

Max got up and said, "Sorry to spoil the celebration."

As he walked to the car Maria called out, "Next time take your sister's advice and leave your MiNDi in your hotel room."

The car drove off with Max and we all just stared at it. Then Maria stood up and said, "If you'll excuse me, I better get on this right away. Don't worry. I'm sure Guardian Security can pull some strings and get Max out in no time. They're indebted to us. Kharis, what was the name of that agent you told me about?"

"Jack. But I don't remember his last name," Kharis asked.

"Then I better get over to Guardian Security's office and see if I can track him down," Maria said.

"Do you want me to come with you? You've never been there and they don't know who you are," Kharis offered.

"That would be helpful if you don't mind," Maria said.

Kharis got up and said, "Well, that was the shortest party I've ever been to. Sorry Dave and Monika. Maybe we can reschedule this when Proxy comes back to town."

"Don't worry about it. But do you have any idea what are they questioning him about?" I asked.

"Haven't you seen today's news?" Kharis asked.

"No, I haven't," I answered.

Kharis pulled out his MiNDi and showed me a couple of headlines: "Russian medical company suspected in sabotage of Future Health's generators," "FSB allegedly complicit in multiple Moscow murders."

"So do the police suspect that Proxy leaked the story to the press?" I asked.

"I'm sure that's what they want to question him about," Kharis said.

"Did he really do it?" Monika asked.

Kharis grinned, "Yes, he did. But they'll never be able to prove it. They just want to scare him."

"I doubt they'll succeed with that," I said.

"No, probably not." Kharis said as he and Maria got up to leave. "Well, you two go ahead and enjoy a quiet breakfast on your own. It's already paid for," Kharis said.

"Thanks, Kharis. I guess we will."

"Have you decided if you want to come to church tomorrow?" he asked.

Monika looked at me and asked, "Can we?"

I said to Kharis, "We'd like that. Just let us know where and when."

"Good. I'll call you later."

Maria said, "Dave, we really appreciate all that you've done. And I would like for all of us to get together again when Max is back in town. I'll be in touch."

"We'll look forward to it," I said.

After they left Monika and I enjoyed a nice leisurely breakfast together. When we finished I said, "Let's go home and pack up the bikes and take them to the river trail for a ride."

"That sounds like fun. But after all the riding you've been doing lately, I doubt I'll be able to keep up with you."

"We'll keep it short, I promise."

We got into the car and as we were driving home Hailey announced, "Good morning, Dave. Your Net Connex notification system has sent you a message: You are out of milk."

I groaned. Monika laughed and asked, "So are you ready to give me a chance to fix the fridge?"

"Sure. Be my guest."

www.ingramcontent.com/pod-product-compliance
Lightning Source LLC
Chambersburg PA
CBHW020406150626
46554CB00012B/385